A MAN WITHOUT FEAR

Massey waited, and watched him. Then, slowly and deliberately, he raised his revolver and covered the forehead of Calmont.

"I should have done it long ago," he said. "It's not a crime. It's a good thing to put a cur like you out of the world. You're a fiend. You're a cold-blooded snake, Calmont. You tried to murder me. Now I'm going to do justice on you."

"Hugh! Hugh!" I shouted. "It's murder!"

"Shut up and keep away from me!" said Massey, as cold as steel.

Calmont, in the meantime, did not beg for his life, did not flinch. I never hope to see such a thing again. He merely leaned a bit forward and looked with his usual sneering smile into the eye of the revolver, exactly like a man staring at a camera when his picture is about to be taken. His color did not alter. There was no fear in Arnold Calmont when he looked death in the face, and that is a thing worth remembering.

MAX BRAND

SIXTEEN IN NOME

LEISURE BOOKS NEW YORK CITY

A LEISURE BOOK®

February 1999

Published by special arrangement with Golden West Literary Agency.

Dorchester Publishing Co., Inc.
276 Fifth Avenue
New York, NY 10001

An earlier version of this novel appeared in installments in *Western Story Magazine* and acknowledgment is made to Condé Nast Publications, Inc.

ISBN 0-8439-4486-2

SIXTEEN IN NOME

Chapter One
Nome

Once a hardy old-timer in a mangy parka said to me: "I'd rather be barefoot in the desert than sixteen in Nome." The point was that I was sixteen, and in Nome at that moment, and without needing the slightest time for consideration, I agreed with him.

Sixteen is a bad age for a boy. It is too full of growing and not full enough of strength. I looked big enough but I was pretty soft. My hands and feet would not do what I wanted them to. My body, my mind, my spirits had not settled down enough.

Take a lad who's been raised in a fishing smack or ridden the Montana range in winter as a regular thing, and he would have done pretty well, even in Nome. But I had done none of those things. I had worked with cows a little in Arizona. I could daub on a rope, and even use a branding iron, but I did not excel in anything. With a rifle, for instance, I was a pretty good hand—every boy on the Arizona range is. With a revolver I was no good

7

at all. The mere feel of a horse arching its back frightened me numb and, as for wrestling, boxing, and such things, I knew very little about them. I was simply an overgrown youth with a skinny neck and a large Adam's apple and, in Nome, a perpetual shudder at the cold.

Nome would have been a depressing place for older and stronger people than I. The ugly beach, spotted with the holes of the mines, the rocks, the high tundra edge, the sod houses, the unwashed crowds of men, the snarling, howling dogs by day and night, the cold, the wind, the storms, the brawlers in the streets, the bitter hardness of the work, and the scant amount of it that I found to do used to make me sit down and beat my knuckles against my face sometimes, and wonder how I could have been so foolish. There was that good, comfortable, little Arizona shack, and the good hot sun, and the sounds of cattle lowing and coyotes yipping on the edge of the sky—a medley that seemed to me like heaven on this morning when I crawled out of my bunk in the Tucker Lodging House. There were half a dozen people getting up at the same time in the same room. The air was foul and close; men were groaning as they got into their shoes. Their eyes were swollen with sleep and the aftereffects of cheap whisky which they had had the night before. And everyone in that wretched room seemed almost as miserable as I.

But I knew that they were not what they seemed. In a few minutes their strong bodies would be warmed by speeding blood, their heads would be high, and their shoulders back; and they would be heartened, also, by the knowledge that they had money in their pockets, or, at least, jobs to go to. I had neither.

In the last three days, I had eaten once, and it was thirty-six hours since I had tasted a morsel. Thirty-six hours is not much to a man, but to a growing boy it is thirty-six hours of anguish. I had suffered, and suffered badly. I expected to suffer still more, but pride kept me from going in the evening to The Joint, where ''Doctor'' Borg never failed to hand out at least a dollar to every mendicant.

As I dressed, my depression grew. The fingers with which I buttoned my shirt were grimy. I told myself that I had sunk so low that even personal cleanliness no longer was attractive or necessary to me. I said to myself that I was slipping into the out tide and would soon be lost.

The lodging house of Mr. Tucker seemed more disagreeable than ever this morning. It was built by him according to a plan of his own, of which he was so proud that he was never done talking of it. It seemed a very good plan, too, and neat. He got a number of ten-by-twelve tents and put them side by side. Over each tent he nailed boards, so that it turned into a sort of box. Over the outside of the boards he stacked up thick walls of sod. The result was a house with a number of rooms, and enough weight of walls to make it seem secure against the cold. But the sods had been put on when they were frozen. They never had a good chance to thaw and compact, and the result was that the arctic cold was able to work its skinny fingers through and get at every living thing in the Tucker House.

Tucker himself would not admit that he felt the cold. He was so proud of the new scheme of building he had invented, and he was so delighted with himself for having had such a grand idea that I've actually seen him going around in his shirt sleeves, with only a light sweater, through these rooms. The couple inches of fat which he wore under his hide could not insulate him against the cold of the Far North; his skin used to turn blue and his eyes bulged, but he insisted that his was the warmest house in Nome.

By the time I had dressed, this morning, my spirits were at zero. My fingers were numb. My stomach was as empty as that of any soaring vulture. As I started for the door, I heard one of the men say: "That kid is broke and about starved."

This made me walk more slowly, and my mouth fairly watered with hope; but the man's partner said to him: "Don't be a fool. The kid's a bum, and we ain't any too flush."

"Yeah. You've said it right," said the first man, and I walked on into the hallway.

I went by a doorway inside which a pair of men were cursing each other in voices that reached up the scale and told that blows were coming, but I had seen so much fighting in Nome that I was not interested enough to stop and inquire about it or wait to hear the scrap begin. Fist fights were a drug on the market in the Nome streets, where five thousand wastrels and unemployed tumbled and fought like sea gulls for the scraps that fell from the fat tables of the land.

A few steps farther, I heard a woman crying on a deep, moaning note and, through the flimsy door, distinctly, I could hear the sound of blows against flesh. Either some brute of a man was beating her, or else she was striking her own breast.

Now, weakened as I was, and in that horrible atmosphere, it made me a little sick. I stopped and leaned against the wall, with my head spinning. A couple of men pressed by me, heard the sounds inside the room, and went by, grinning to one another.

This beastliness in human nature then took me by the throat and gave me a shake, as it were. My circulation picked up, and I got so strong that I tapped on that door, and then pushed it open. If there were a man inside, I would be beaten to a pulp, but I had a curious, starved desire to tell him what I thought of his brutality.

There was no man inside.

There was only a red-headed girl sitting on the side of her bunk and swaying backward and forward, with her head thrown back, and her hands whacking against her chest, now and then. From a husky, deep pitch of her voice, I had taken her to be a woman of middle age. But she was only a girl of twenty or nineteen.

This made a tremendous difference. The horror went a pair of octaves up the scale. I closed the door behind me, and the squeak of the hinges, this time, made her start up.

She asked me what I wanted, while I stared at her, for a moment, through the wretched gloom of that half light. This red-headed girl was not a beauty, but she was good looking. Even through that twilight I was struck by the deep blue of her eyes. She had a bit too much mouth and not quite enough chin, but she was decidedly what one would call a pretty girl.

I told her that I wanted nothing, except to stop her crying, if I could.

"You're going to stop it, are you?" asked the girl in a dry way—but with a sob or two bubbling up.

"I will if I'm able to be any good for you," I told her.

She came up to me and took me by the shoulders—she was just my height—and backed me around until what light there was came bang into my face.

"You're going to help me!" she said.

The sneer in her voice did not bother me. I had had too many of the same sort of sneers thrown my way since I came North, and now I took them for granted.

11

"I'll do what I can," I said. "I know that I'm no Calmont or Massey."

Calmont, do you see, was the strongest man in Nome, people said. And Massey was a bouncer down at The Joint, and said to be the slickest gunman around those parts, where everybody packed a Colt.

"Sonny," said the redhead, "if you were Calmont and Massey rolled into one, you wouldn't be able to help me. Run along now and forget me. It looks as though you've something of your own to think about."

She said that and put her hand right on my stomach. I mean, where my stomach should have been, but it was gone, and the sharp edges of my ribs stood out like the tops of a corral fence all around that cave in the middle of me.

"That ought to be full," she observed to me. "Who stole your insides, mister?"

I felt like a fool. I'd been talking rather big, the moment before, and now she was asking me why I was starved.

"Aw, I'm all right," I told her. "If you're dead sure that I can't do you any good. . . ."

I got back to the door.

"Wait a minute, Sammy. . . ."

"My name's not Sammy," I said.

"What is it, then? Joe?"

"Yes," I said, surprised. "It's Joe. How did you guess that? Do you know that I'm Joe May?"

She laughed a little at me. She seemed to forget a part of her troubles.

"I know it now, anyway, Joe May," she said. "Look. Here's something that will round you out a little. . . ."

She held out ten dollars in gold to me. And my hand jumped for it like a hungry dog for a bone. I had the tips of my fingers on it before I got hold of myself and snatched my hand back. I had been worn down to such a point that I would have taken charity from a man, I think, but to take it from a girl whose eyes were still red with crying was too much for me.

She came after me, offering the money again.

"You take it, Joe," she said. "It'll be between the two of us. You can depend on me not to talk about it, and you're as welcome to it as the flowers in . . . May!"

She laughed again, but there was a choked note in her laughter that about finished me. I did not dare to stay there before her. The two five-dollar pieces looked to me like two glorious suns. Twenty meals lay in the hollow of her hand, and I felt as though I could eat them at one sitting. So I did the only thing that occurred to me. I jerked the door open and got into the hall away from temptation.

Chapter Two
Trouble Comes on Fours

When I got outside of the lodging house, I found that a wind was blowing. It came off the tundra. That is to say, it was full of teeth and fingers of ice, and those fingers were poked between my ribs and into my vitals in a way that made me blink and bite my lip.

I dodged back into the doorway to catch my breath, but I knew that if I remained there for long, I would slink off to my bunk once more and lie in a stupor of misery all day long, as I had done most of the day before. So I got myself together, what there was of me, and turned the corner into the full stroke of the wind.

It was early in the day, there was little light, and what there was of it was smudged away to dusk by a thick sheeting of clouds that lay solidly across the sky. There were few people on that street and, when I turned down into the next one—hardly knowing where I went and hardly caring—I saw not a human soul, only half a dozen big huskies which were roaming to find any scraps of food or trouble that would come their way.

They had that big-shouldered, wolfish look which told me they were inside dogs, the kind that dog-punchers like to have in a team and, by the way they packed together, I could see that they were all from one team. It meant something, if six fine fellows like these were loose in a town where dogs were worth a good deal of money. I wondered how they had come adrift, but there were a good many possible explanations for that. A knife stroke or a bullet might have tipped their master on his face in the snow. Such things happened every day in Nome, at that happy time in its history.

There was a reward in the offing, no matter what had happened, if I could get hold of that half dozen and keep them until called for, which was sure to be before long. However, they were as wolfish in nature as in looks. They showed me their teeth as they went by, and hardly turned out of their tracks to give me room.

I saw that I was helpless, and groaned. More meals were walking away from me. I began to feel that bad luck was represented in everything that was around me, and that I had been led to Nome to enjoy a first install-ment of it.

Another dog, just then, climbed over a fence and jumped down into the snow. He was a beautiful fellow, very tall and with promising points, though he had not yet quite filled out. He was completely white except that the tip of his tail, his ears, and his muzzle had been rubbed with soot, as it were. He was dazzling bright, otherwise, but the odd markings gave him a rather queer look. Of course, I knew him at a glance. Everybody in Nome knew him. That was Alexander the Great, Mas-sey's dog, on account of which Massey and Calmont, every one said, had dissolved their old partnership and now hated each other with a flaming and inextinguishable rage. That was one of the talking points in Nome, that season, and particularly how Doctor Borg had sworn the two men to a truce at the very time when Massey managed to get the dog for him.

The reason that my heart jumped so high was because I knew that that trick dog had been rated as high as five or even seven thousand dollars in value. He performed to a crowd every day in The Joint, like a high-grade vaudevillian, and men used to throw him money and cheer him and fight to get close and pat his clever head.

Well . . . if I could manage to get a hold of Alec the Great without having my hand bitten off, Massey would give me anything that I asked. Yes, or more than I had the nerve to ask! I looked up and down the street again, shuddering for fear any one else might be in sight to rob me of that golden opportunity, but I could see no one.

The next moment there was a terrific yowling and snarling.

I jumped around and, with a start I saw that I was very unlikely to get my hands on Alexander the Great. Neither was Massey, for that matter. And the crowd at The Joint would look for Alec the Great in vain, unless something strange happened.

For the six huskies of that errant dog team just then had come up with the dog and decided, apparently, that they were hungry, and that this was a good meal for them all. There was no hanging back among them. They got into a flying wedge faster than any football team, and then made for Alec in a single lump. They ran low. They ran hard. They were only worried about one thing, and that was how they were going to get all their teeth into him at once.

My blood stopped running and I forgot the cold as I saw Alec look back at that fence and decide that it was too high to be jumped.

What could he do?

He was fairly cornered, and he knew it, but he made a little jump to one side and then to the other. I saw that wave of dog flesh close on him—no, not quite! It was at the very last moment that he tried a most surprising thing. I don't suppose that anything but a man-educated trick dog would have dreamed of such a thing, but Alec thought of it. At the final instant, when the eyes of the huskies were probably blind with the foretaste of a good dinner, Alec left the snow like a bird and sailed high into the air.

He left the leaders so fast that they did not even lift their heads, but a couple of old stagers in the rear reached for him. He was too high and traveling too fast. His jump fairly carried him over the dogs.

His momentum was gone as he landed. He scratched to get footing, and found, that treacherous instant, that he was standing on smoothest ice! A partial thaw, there in the middle of the street, had turned the surface to glass, and Alec floundered like a fish out of water.

The huskies had not stopped against the fence. They did not stop to shake their heads and call themselves fools, as men would have done. They simply hit that fence with all four feet and rebounded halfway across the street, and almost on top of Alec.

I thought that he would do some other clever trick, but it jumped smack into my mind then that there were no more tricks up his sleeve. He had nothing but his four legs under him to save him now, and he tried to use them; but the treacherous surface was much harder on him than it was on the dog team, practiced as they constantly were in going over even worse stuff than this.

I thought that he might get across the street and jump the board fence behind me. But no. That was too high for him, even higher than the opposite one!

As I looked at that fence, I saw that one of the boards was a little broken, and wrenched at it. The major portion of it did not give at all, but I pulled away a sizable club! That gave me an idea and a tenth part of a hope.

Alec seemed to know what was in my mind. He came straight in for me and got behind my legs, while I whirled up that club and gave the leader of the pack a good slam with it across the head. He was coming in so hard that his weight shot ahead after the blow, and he crashed me back against the fence. I thought I was going down. Prickles of ice shot all through me. Once down before a gang like these half-wolves, and they would have an easier throat than Alec's to cut.

However, the swing of that stick and the splintering sound of the blow split the charge in two sections that sheered off from me to either side, and Alec woke up the stunned leader at my feet with a slash that opened the whole side of his shoulder. No mustang ever jumped faster and further than that dog did under the spur of Alec's stroke.

I looked down and saw Alec grinning back to me, a red-stained smile. I swung the club, and shouted, but when the other dogs jumped away, the injured leader simply snarled and came in a slinking pace toward me.

There is a good deal of evil in most huskies. The wolf strain is strong in them and, though on the whole they are willing to admit that a man with a club or a whip in his hands is the master, still they're liable to play mean tricks. I did not know their language, either, or the proper way to curse them out with a choice sprinkling of Eskimo words, say.

That big warrior seemed to guess at once that I was not the sort of iron he had found in men before me. I think about the worst thing I ever saw in my life was the long, gliding step that he made at me as I swung that club and shouted.

The rest of the team needed no better hint than this. In one jump they were back on each flank of him, eyeing me, pressing in close to the fence. One of them was snarling softly. The rest of them were silent, however, and that hungry silence meant a good deal more than growls at me.

I forgot about reclaiming dogs, rewards, and all that sort of thing. I began to yell at the top of my lungs for help. Not far away—in the next street, perhaps, I heard a number of men begin to laugh. Suddenly I realized that people did not turn out of their way in Nome to pay attention to the first yelping they heard, whether it came from dogs or men. The social instincts of a pack of wolves were almost kind compared to the instincts of that crowd, taking it by and large.

A frightful feeling of helplessness came over me. I got faint, and my breath would not come. I waved the club and whirled it in the air again.

The big leader slid forward on his belly like a stalking cat, and curled his lips away from his teeth. I decided it would have to be then or never. The whole of that horrible semicircle had drawn suddenly in around me and I knew, that unless I made some move, it would most likely be the end of me. So I feinted. He dodged his head a little, and then I let him have it alongside the head.

The club broke off short in my hand. The crackling and the stroke itself made the younger dogs of the team wince away a trifle; but, as for that leader, it was as though I had hit him with a feather duster. He simply showed me his teeth and the darkness inside his throat as he came excitedly off the ground at me.

Now, as that big brute began to rise, I told myself that

it was the end. The horror and the fear weakened my arms to nothing at all. I could not have dodged and I could not have struck a single worthwhile blow with the truncheon of the stick.

It was young Alec the Great who saved me. He went past my legs in a flash. The leader had been thinking only of the human enemy and, as a result, just as he came off the ground Alec's shoulder hit him and tumbled him head over heels with a rip down the side that spurted red.

There was a clear field for Alec, through that gap, and he could have bolted, but that did not seem to occur to him. Instead, he flashed back to my side instantly.

There was one bad moment when I thought that the team would rush me from either side but, like well-trained workers, they waited for orders from that ugly gray brute; and he had something new to think about.

The second blow, the second ripping stroke, apparently had brought him to his senses. Perhaps the battle had only started as a frolic. Perhaps he had gone blindly on from chasing a mere dog to attacking a man, and now he suddenly realized that he had been trying to pull down a human, and that man's medicine is usually strong. At any rate, he gave us one wicked side glance, and then went off down the street. The rest of his crew tailed along after him like privates after a corporal. I never was so glad to see dogs going the other way.

Chapter Three
Massey, Master of Alec

Looking after them, with my eyes fairly popping, and the reeling dizziness only gradually working out of my head, I kept reaching down and patting Alec the Great, for as the huskies jogged away, I could think again about Alec.

Rewards were not in my mind, however. You don't think of rewards from any creature that has been through the fear of death with you. It was reasonably true that I had saved him from being mobbed—as I thought then—but it seemed equally true that he had saved me from a pretty pickle.

I made another pat for the head of Alec and found that he was not there. He had run off a little way down the street and was fawning around a man who was in the act of putting away a revolver inside his coat.

You can imagine that I stared at him. For suddenly I realized that I had not been alone and helpless during this fracas. That fellow must have been there a good part of it. He had pulled out a revolver to intervene if necessary. But he had not fired.

The cold-bloodedness of this staggered me. I had been a twentieth part of a second from having my throat ripped wide open, when the leader started to spring; and still the man had not fired, or rushed in with so much as a shout, but in a calm silence he had stood off there and watched the wrangle.

There was still a smile on his face, so that I knew he had been enjoying the little battle as if it had been staged for fun.

His face was pretty well muffled in fur cheek flaps, but I could see that he was young, and that he had a pair of eyes as hard and cold as the light that gleams on a steadied rifle barrel. He was not the sort of a man that one would reproach about anything, not unless one wanted either a fight or chilly contempt. I have seen that look in the faces of a few other men, and always they are the fellows who have been at danger's door and had a good chance to admire the interior.

He came up to me while I was still agape. "Who are you?" he said.

I started to answer, but the cold, the relief from terrible danger, and the sense of uncanny awe that was in me made my lips too stiff for words.

It was only after a second effort that I managed to say: "I'm Joe May."

"You'd better go home and put on something warm!" said this fellow. "Got no more sense than to come out in that sort of rig?"

There was so grimly commanding an air about him that I muttered something and turned on my heel and did as he had told me to do. I was too numbed in the brain not to do as he commanded, for I realized that this was no other than the great Massey himself. That being so, it explained why he ventured to stand by and reserve his fire until the last split part of a second, for they said that he was one of those men who cannot miss.

It no longer seemed strange to me that he had not offered any reward for the care I had taken of Alec. As a matter of fact, Alec had taken just about as much care of me! However, Massey had the reputation of being a fellow who cared for only two things in the world— Alec the Great and fighting. He was not the one, I supposed, to bother about sentimental payments such as charity to a ragged kid he had run into on the street.

I went back to the lodging house, therefore, simply because I saw that there was nothing else for me to do. I was paid up until that night, and at least I could keep the gnawing, painful, bitter spark of life alive in my breast until that time, lying crouched under my blankets.

So I went down the dark, cold dampness of the hall-way and came again to the room where I had spent the night. Despair came over me as I entered that room, and the rank foulness of the air struck me in the face. Let them tell of the good, brave days of Alaska, but ah, the horrible pain I have known there.

I got to the bunk, but did not lie down at once. Instead, I sat on the edge of it with my face in my hands and my closed eyes looking at death, which I hoped would not be far away. Out of the naked earth of the floor, I felt the cold pass up into my feet, and higher, until my ankles ached. And I calmly wondered if it would not be better, really, to get to the outer margin of the town and simply lie down in the snow.

Of all deaths, it is the sweetest. I had heard it described. The pangs of the cold soon pass. There comes a delicious, an enormous wave of drowsiness. Pleasant thoughts move warmly through the soul. And that is the end. It is exactly like dropping off to sleep in a warm bed.

At this moment, a stone was dropped into the stagnant pool of my life. The harsh voice of a man spoke to me from the doorway.

"Going to lie down and die like a sick puppy?" asked that voice.

I looked vaguely, without resentment, toward the form in the doorway. There was no pride in me to bruise. I was only sixteen, and I had been pretty well rubbed down to the core.

A wet nose touched my hand. It was Alec the Great, and I saw that Massey had followed me home.

"Have you paid your room rent?" he asked me.

"Yes," I said.

"Are those your blankets?"

"No."

"Get up, then, and follow me out of this pigsty."

I got up without a word and walked at his heels down the hallway and, when we came out into the street, I still floundered at his heels, blindly, like a dog behind a master. In some manner, the question of the future had been slipped onto his shoulders. He would have to solve it, and numbly I rejoiced at getting rid of the weight. This is not a heroic admission, but it is the truth. An empty stomach, I have found, is a famous corrupter of both pride and virtue.

We went down the street through the snow for a way, then he stopped, took me by the shoulder, and gave me a hard shake. I was loose in his grasp, which was like iron.

"Stand up beside me and walk out like a man!" said he. "Don't trail at my heels like a beaten cur!"

That was a little too much. The words, you might say,

tilted back my head and threw up my chin like a straight left to the button.

"I'm not asking your advice about how I walk!" I said.

His gleaming, steady eyes looked through me like a glancing knife blade. A sneer formed on his lips, and disappeared slowly.

"Then hold up your head and walk beside me," he said.

I did as I was told. But anger was beginning to warm me inwardly. I set my teeth hard and strode along. I wondered if I should challenge him to a fight. At least, my pride was now not quite dead.

A little farther along, we were met by a man who was running at full speed, head down. When he saw Massey, he halted with a jerk.

"Massey!" he said. "Did you see my string of dogs?"

Massey answered not a word. He walked straight on and, when I would have blundered out an answer, Massey took me by the arm and dragged me forward.

I saw that the other fellow was gaping angrily after us, on the verge of shouting an insult which he controlled. Men did not shout insults at Massey. Not in Nome, where they had cause to know him. Half a dozen gunmen had started to make a reputation at his expense at one time or another, and they had all become mere footnotes in the story of his life.

But this little incident started me wondering what was wrong with the master of Alec. I could see that he was wearing a grim little smile, as though he actually had had a touch of enjoyment out of keeping back information from that dog-puncher.

I wonder if it were mere justice—punishment for a man who had allowed his team to get loose and thereby had endangered the life of the great Alec, who was more valuable than five times the entire lot? But it seemed to me that it was no mere matter of justice. Something more was involved. There was the question of that cruel, cold little smile.

I had heard, as every one in Nome had, the terrible tale of how Massey and Calmont had lived together until they hated one another because of Alec. They had been old, tried, proven friends. They had gone through everything together. Life and honor and everything they had owed to one another repeatedly. I could not help wondering, as I slipped and skidded on the icy snow crust beside Massey, if something had gone out of this man's life because of that breach between him and his old friend. Stranger things than that have happened. However, certainly I never met a man who, at first glance, appeared to be so entirely devoid of the ordinary gentler human emotions.

I was to know him much better and, the longer I knew him, the stranger the picture of him became. There was enough here to look at from a thousand angles, but never enough to show me the entire man. You would have said that he possessed some great secret on which he had locked his lips and which the world could never get at. For my own part, I am convinced that it was the wound made when he found his old partner and bunkie untrue to him. Enough to make even a saint put on a bit of a shell, I should say.

All these thoughts were struggling through my brain as I marched up the street beside him.

We turned a corner. A gust of icy wind struck strongly at me. I staggered. My feet went out from under me, and I fell flat. There was a solid whack about that fall, and I lay limp for a moment until I heard the harsh voice of Massey calling out:

"Pick yourself up! If you're not able to do that, you're not able to live, anyway, and I'll be hanged if you're worth wasting time over!"

I got to my feet, somehow, though now between cold and hunger and utter weakness I was pretty far spent. But the anger swallowed my other sensations. That fellow Massey had deliberately walked on ahead of me after his last remark, and I hated him with a power that gave me strength.

I ran after him. I shouted.

He pretended not to hear, or else the whistling of the wind may have drowned my words.

At last I stumbled up to him at the door of a sod house and touched his shoulder.

"I want to tell you," I shouted at him, "that I don't want your help! You and your help can both be hanged!" I yelled at him and shook a blue hand in his face.

He kicked open the door. He took me by the shoulder, and I still can see the sneer on his face as he hurled me before him into the room.

Chapter Four

For a Stake

When I had stumbled into that one-room house, Massey entered and locked the door behind him. I was still hot and angry. I turned around and began to demand that the door should be opened, but he paid no attention to me whatever. The smell of food, too, was making my mouth water, and inside that house it was quite snug, for a fire had been banked down in the stove in the center of the room.

No palace ever looked to me as comfortable as the inside of that place. There were two bunks, though only one had blankets on it, but such a heap as might have served for three beds instead of one, it seemed to me. From pegs on the wall hung enough clothes to keep half a regiment warm. Good, strong boots were lined up underneath, and soft slippers for tired feet to take their ease in. Over in a corner provisions were heaped. I smelled ham, bacon, the perfume of dried fruits, and I could see the delicious labels of canned jams and jellies. These

28

were tremendous luxuries. But all I could think of, just then, was a fine, fat slice of bacon and a chunk of bread, washed down with tea. The mere mental picture of such a feast made me fairly dizzy.

I slumped into a chair and waited there, watching Massey with haunted eyes. I got almost exactly what I wanted, but in the meantime some interesting things happened.

Massey pulled off his heavy coat and furred cap and the long boots. The dog took those things one by one and carried them across to a bench beside the wall pegs. The way he handled that big, ponderous coat was a caution. He gave it a flip and threw it across his shoulder, the way a fox will carry a heavy goose, and he unloaded it carefully on the bench. The unloading was harder than the carrying. A sleeve or a flap of it kept sliding off. The thing seemed to be made of sand, the way it kept running down toward the floor.

But Alec kept after it. He got so impatient and excited that he bounced up and down and whined, but finally he had that coat duly tucked away in place.

Back he raced for the cap and snatched that away to the bench, then took the boots both at once—a tag in either side of his mouth—and dragged them off to the line. He took something with him on each return journey—a sort of pull-over knitted cap for the head, a light jacket, and that pair of loose, soft slippers which I've spoken of before.

I suppose that a thousand dogs have been trained by patience and some skill to do much harder tricks than these, and afterward I saw Alec do infinitely more difficult things, but nothing in the animal world ever impressed me more than this housekeeping by a dog, and the joy and shining eyes and wagging tail with which he went about it. I found that I had forgotten all about my grievances against Massey, and that I was looking across to him with a smile and an overflowing warmth of heart. His own face, however, showed not the slightest relaxation. It was like ice.

"Pull off those shoes," he directed. I obeyed dumbly. "Are your feet frozen? Get that brown coat and put it on. Here's a pair of socks. Pull off those wet things and put on these. And here's a pair of slippers."

I still obeyed. My pride was in my pocket. Besides, I was telling myself that Alec the Great had never been trained by cruelty, and that a man who had done so much with a dog by patient gentleness could not be the cold-hearted brute he wanted to appear to men.

I had enough strength, now, to get up and stamp my feet to help the circulation along, and I began to feel a lot better, though just a bit shaky in the knees.

Massey had the fire built up by this time. The crackling of it, the fuming of the smoke through the crack, the tremor and the roar of the draft up the chimney, sounded a great deal sweeter to me than any chorus of Christmas hymns. He put on the kettle of water to boil, and sliced some great pieces of bacon into a frying pan. Then he made a flapjack by pouring water into the top of a flour sack after he had mixed in some salt and baking powder. In this way he composed a great ball of dough, which was fried out in the bacon fat and turned brown there. So I had exactly what I wanted—bacon, fried bread, and a quantity of tea.

It did not occur to me at the time, but now I can remember that Massey hardly touched the food. He pretended that he had been cooking for us both, but really he had been cooking for me only.

When I was warm and full inside, then I began to pay more attention to my host. I cared less about his harsh words and gestures, now. To a boy, actions mean a great deal more than words, and all Massey's actions had been kind. Besides, he was famous, and he was a mystery. Every moment I grew more deeply and affectionately interested in him.

"What brought you to Alaska?" he asked me.

I considered. And then I felt like a fool as I answered: "Well, I wanted to make some money."

"Have you?" he asked in the same unrelenting tone.

That certainly was an unnecessary question. Tears stung my eyes suddenly, so that I had to scowl as I answered: "You can see for yourself."

"Where'd you come from?" he asked me.

"Arizona."

"Where you going?"

"I don't know what you mean."

"On to Russia, or back to Arizona?"

I set my teeth. "Not back to Arizona. Not yet."

"When?"

"When I can show something more than my face."

"When you can come back rich, eh?"

Well, as I watched his sneer it occurred to me that he was not sneering at me alone, but at all humanity, including himself. There was a sort of general disbelief in him concerning every one and everything. This made it less of a personal insult. I could talk straight out at him seriously, with a vague belief that under the surface this man was good and kind.

Goodness and kindness matter most to hungry young boys and wise old men, it appears to me. In the stage in between, were more interested in smartness and strength.

"Maybe I won't be rich. I just want a stake," I said.

"For what?" he snapped.

"To get a piece of ground and a few cows."

"That your ambition?"

"It doesn't sound much," I admitted, "but it's the life that I want to have ahead of me."

"A shack to live in, and a couple of mustangs to ride, and a couple of dozen mangy cows to herd around?" he suggested.

"A herd that'll grow, and time to grow it in," I said, "and to be my own boss. That's what I want. And to see my own land, and to ride on it. Put up my own fences. Break my own horses. Brand my own cattle. Have some good shooting, now and then. Get some bounties on coyote scalps. Trap a wolf or two. I know it doesn't sound much, but there's more fun on the range than you can shake a stick at."

He turned his back on me and rattled at the stove. Suddenly he astonished me by saying: "Aye, that's what I'd like to do, also. And here I am in Nome."

"What for?" I asked.

"For a stake," he said.

He turned and surprised me more than ever with a broad grin. But he made no further comment on me or on himself. He simply said: "You better turn in and sleep till you've digested that meal. Have you got a mother and a father alive?"

"Yes," I said.

"Do they know where you are?"

"They've an idea."

"Well, you turn in and sleep," he repeated.

And he fixed some blankets on the second bunk for me.

I did as he said, and by the time I had stretched myself out, I was dead to the world. I had done my share of sleeping in the days that went just before, but starvation sleep means miserable nightmares. This time, I dropped away into a happy land.

I dreamed that I had gone into a country where the

dogs talked English, and where the king of the dogs was all white except for a smutty tip to his tail and ears and muzzle. I woke up finally, and found that Alec the Great was sitting beside my bunk with his bright eyes only inches from my face. He grinned at me as only a dog can, and then I sat up and looked around me.

The world looked pretty good, I can tell you.

I had lain down as gorged as a snake, but now I was hungry again. The strength was back in my knees. There was contentment in my mind. I looked upon Massey as my savior, and that is what he was. It never occurred to me that in meeting him I *was* meeting the wildest adventures of my life.

I got up and walked around the cabin. I picked up a rifle in the corner and admired the make of it. I stopped to admire the little stove, too, and then put more wood in it. It was one of the traveling variety, which will fold up small enough to put in your pocket, almost, but which shed enough heat to warm up a barn.

Massey, I decided, was a man who knew his business. If a fellow like him could not make a stake in Nome, nobody could, except some fool with beginner's luck, perhaps. While I was in the midst of these wanderings, I came to the place where his clothes were hanging and touched a jacket.

A deep snarl from Alec the Great warned me that I had stepped across my bounds. That young dog was crouched and showing his teeth at me in the true husky style. But I did not argue. He was watching his master's things, and I admired him for it. Such a dog I never had seen, and such a dog I never will see again!

After a little while, Massey came back. He said to me: "How are things with you now?"

"I'm fine," I said.

"I've got to go to work," he told me. "My job is at

The Joint, and Alec goes with me. Do you play cards?"

"Not for money."

"Do you drink?"

"Not yet."

"Then you'd better come along with me," he said. "Mind you, in The Joint, keep your ears open and your mouth shut. There'll be plenty to see and hear, but nothing worth answering back or repeating. You understand?"

"Yes," I said, my eyes beginning to open.

And that was how I went with him to The Joint, which was the great beginning, for me.

Chapter Five
Between Dog and Master

So many people have heard of The Joint that there's no use in describing its three great rooms or the crowd in them. It averaged, I suppose, the toughest lot of men ever gathered together evening by evening, in any part of the world, at any time in the world's history.

My own first impression was a tangled one of wild eyes and wild faces seen through swirls of cigarette and cigar and pipe smoke. Music screeched and throbbed and groaned in the dance hall adjoining, but Massey had sent me to a corner table of the main barroom, and there I kept my place, and my eyes grew so big that they ached as I watched the movements in the throng.

The place was pretty well packed. At every second or third table there was a card game with raw gold piled up for stakes, and raw whisky at every table to encourage a liberal spirit among the gamesters. After I had been in my chair for a time, a waiter came by and asked what I would have, and I said that I was only waiting.

He seemed amazed. He put his fists on his hip bones and glared at me.

"You're only waitin', are you?" he said. "There ain't any waitin' in The Joint, you loony. There's only comin' and goin'."

He hooked his finger over his shoulder, and I stood up to go. But go where?

Massey had told me to sit at that table and not to budge, and much as I dreaded that long, lanky, formidable waiter, I dreaded Massey a good deal more.

"Hump along, kid, hump along," he said, with another jerk of his thumb.

"But Massey told me to wait here," I explained timidly.

The waiter was amazed.

"Massey? Hugh Massey?" he said.

"Yes," I said.

"I'm gunna find out dang pronto," declared the waiter, "and if it's a lie, you'll go through that door on your head!"

He retired. Two men at the next table laughed jeeringly at me, and I shrank smaller and smaller in my chair.

Presently, as I looked about the room, I saw Massey himself walking toward me, and I heaved a great sigh of relief. But he seemed to be paying no attention to me. He was following Alec the Great, who wandered along between the tables looking with an almost human intelligence into the faces of the men.

I could hear them muttering to one another as he went by, and some of the words reached me.

"That's that dang mind-readin' dog," said one of them.

"Mind-readin, and man-killin'," said another.

Then Alec spotted me.

I noticed that every one of those people—even the gamblers in the midst of their hands—looked up and spoke to the dog, but no hand was stretched out to pat him, and he went up to no one. It gave me a little chill of excitement, therefore, when he saw me and came straight to my chair. He put his chin on my knee and I stroked his head, as proud of that sign of acquaintance-ship and friendliness as though a great man had talked to me.

Massey went on without a word of greeting, and the dog went with him, as a matter of course. But that hardly mattered now. For Alec's little call had been enough to identify me as a person of importance, as it were, and the men at the neighboring tables looked at me with a good deal of respect.

One of them with a ten days' beard and an old slouch hat on his head turned in his chair and said: "You're a friend of Massey, kid?"

I nodded. I supposed that I was a friend of Massey's, if a one-day acquaintance could be counted that far.

"Come over here and have a drink," he said, with a smile of invitation.

I told him that I didn't drink, and he remained turned about, staring at me. Finally he began to nod.

"That's right," he said. "Wait till your whiskers be-gin to thicken up a little. This stuff would dissolve tun-dra moss at fifty below. You keep to dogs and Masseys, and leave the liquor alone!"

This remark of his apparently went as a good joke among the others, and they laughed heartily at it. I won-dered if they would have been so free if Massey had been around.

There was plenty to keep my eyes and ears busy, just as Massey had said there would be and, aside from that remark, I did not speak to a soul in the room. The waiter, who evidently had been to Massey and heard enough to put his mind at ease, favored me with a nod and a smile now, as he went by my table. When several men wanted to sit down with me, he warned them off briefly.

"That's Massey's table," he said.

"Why, there's a kid here already," said one of them.

"He belongs to Massey," said the waiter, and there was no further argument.

It did not surprise me, however, that Massey had such power. Every one in Nome had heard more or less about his exploits. And everybody in Nome knew that he was working as a bouncer in The Joint, not so much because of the money he could make there, as because he loved trouble in all its forms.

Later on in the evening, an announcer came through, bawling out that Alexander the Great was going to do a brand-new trick that night. This caused a great commotion, and every one stood up on tables or crowded around the narrow open space which made an aisle down the center of the room.

Half a dozen little stools were put there at a wide distance apart from one another, and then Massey came in with Alec. He announced that Alec would make the trip down the aisle by jumping from one of those stools to the other.

That did not sound very hard until one looked at the tops of the stools and saw that they were hardly six inches in diameter—not room enough for the dog to get all four of his paws on them without crowding his big feet close together.

Alec, when the word was given, had to make three efforts before he managed to get on top of the first stool. There he balanced for a moment, wavering, and half a dozen voices called out, offering bets that he would never complete the trip. The bets were taken, and they ran high. I think one of those silly miners offered five hundred dollars, and was snapped up before the words were out of his mouth.

No stakes were posted. There was not time for that and, besides, even in Nome, there was what one might call "Far Northern" honesty. A man's word was as good as his bond—for a time, at least.

After Alec had regained his balance, he jumped high in the air and came down on the next stool. But though he landed fair and true on the top of it, with his four feet bunched together, the shock of a hundred and twenty pounds of dog skidded that stool across the floor.

Alec staggered on this unstable footing.

He stuck out his head, wavered from side to side, and lost his grip with two feet at once. Luckily, they were on opposite sides. He regained his steady balance and there went up an Indian whoop of triumph from that assembly of miners, thugs, thieves, yeggs, and gamblers.

I noticed that the man who had bet five hundred against the dog yelled more loudly than any one else in praise of Alec's skill. He was certainly a good sport.

Alec went on to the third stool, which did not skid at all, and he immediately leaped again to the fourth, which made a heavy sheer to the left and ahead.

He toppled. I felt sure that he was a goner, but in some manner he managed to right himself.

I heard Massey shout something to him, I couldn't make out what, and Alec gave one small waggle of his tail to show that he had heard. It was like a smile, you might say, from a busy acrobat to a friend in the audience. You could see by the gleaming eyes of Alec that he loved this business.

Off he popped onto the fifth stool, but then a wail of anxiety went up from every one. My own throat ached, and I realized that I had been yelling for Alec all the while. The noise in that place was past belief.

The reason was that the fifth stool skidded not at all, but the solid impact of the dog's weight was too much for it, and one leg crashed.

It knocked Alec completely off balance, of course, but without trying to rebalance himself, like a wise-footed dog on breaking ice, he leaped again, firmly kicking the stool headlong behind him.

His trajectory was low. He hit that sixth stool with a whang and knocked it spinning into the wall.

But by good luck, the turn of the stool allowed him to whang against the wall sideways, and though the shock made him grunt as though he had been kicked by a heavy foot, there he stuck on top of his foothold until the voice of Massey called him down.

He had had such a severe bang that he wobbled a little as he trotted back to Massey.

Every one was shouting and yelling and clapping hands, and in general raising a ruction on account of that dog, and Alec certainly deserved some notice, but what I fastened my attention to was the face of Massey as the dog came up to him.

He looked like cold iron but, just as Alec got to him, I saw for a quarter of a second a single touch of a smile. There was love in that smile. And it reassured me about Massey more than a hundred praises from a hundred men. For I saw that he really loved Alec, and a man who can love a dog cannot really be all bad, or all hard.

When we settled back into our chairs again, there was a great uproar of voices still going on, and everything was in praise of the greatness of Alec. I myself was hoarse from shouting. And I never heard so many fine things said in a short time about any animal—or any man, for that matter! People said that Alec could learn as fast as a human, and it seemed almost true, for he was a very young dog to have such a pocketful of tricks.

That was not the only excitement this evening, however. Not by a jugful!

We had hardly got well quieted down again, and the betting debts paid, when the announcer came in and climbed up on the bar.

He made a speech to us. The speech ran something like this: "Gentlemen, we're pretty far north. Some of you may say that we're too far north for comfort. But what is the major part of a man's comfort? Why, a warm house and a good wife, I suppose."

A few cynical remarks were shouted in answer to this, but the speech was allowed to go on, because the theme promised to be unique.

"Gentlemen," said the announcer, "we're so far north that prices have changed."

"So has the whisky!" some one bawled out.

The announcer was not perturbed. He went on:

"Prices have changed, and a lot of other things have changed, too. There are places down in God's country where wives come cheap. There are places where they can be had for the asking. And there's many a girl that can't even be given away!"

The crowd laughed amiably. They began to feel expectant. Something was coming that was out of the ordinary, or they could be sure that so much preparation would not have preceded it. Effects were not carelessly thrown away in The Joint, or over the varnished surface of the bar so recklessly marred with heel marks.

"But up here in the Far North," said the speaker, "a woman has a good deal of value. Outside of cooking and sewing for a man, she can talk back to him with something more than a bark, and that's all the conversation that a good many of us have six months of the year. Now, boys, even if you were to no more than pay

41

the freight on the shipment of a girl, it would total up
to a tidy lot. Even if you got a hundred and forty pounds
of statue, it would be worth something. So what is a
hundred and forty pounds of lady worth, auctioned off
here in The Joint?''

He made a pause. A yell of excitement followed the
announcement. I listened, but I was not able to believe
my ears.

He continued in the same manner as before:

''Right up here on this bar we're gunna put a girl
who's willing to be auctioned off to the highest bidder
to marry him and be his rightful wife. She's gunna reserve the right to call the deal off if she don't like the
looks of the fellow who bids. That throws him off and
the next highest is in line. But as for the price, she ain't
gunna say a word. She leaves that to you! Cliff, hand
the lady up, will you?''

Chapter Six
Eleven Thousand Bid

I was so amazed that I hunched lower in my chair and gaped like a fish while Cliff Anson, the red-headed chief bartender of The Joint, assisted a girl to climb to the top of the bar.

I was so dazzled by the lights, and by the idea of this transaction, that I could hardly make her out, except that she was dressed in ordinary clothes, without any touch of color to set her off, and her hat was a little toward the back of her head. But I heard a gasp of excitement from the men in that big room, and by this I knew that there was something extraordinary about her.

I rubbed my eyes, looked again, and, by Heaven, it was the red-headed girl whom I had seen crying that same morning in my lodging house! That fairly knocked the breath out of me. It seemed to me that I saw her lighted by the golden glow of the money which she had offered me in her hand not so many hours before. Now

43

she was here, reduced to this. I stared at her with all my heart and soul.

She was trying to smile, but the smile hardly came, and then went again. There was not a speck of rouge on her face, and the result was that she was burning red one minute and white as a ghost the next. I thought she was going to faint, and I was close to it myself, there was something so horrible in this idea. For she was mighty pretty. Even with the tears and all that morning, and the dirty, dusky light of the room against her, she had seemed pretty. But here she shone through the smoke of The Joint by her own light, as it were. She had one hand against her breast, drawing her coat together, and that hand was white enough to have touched the heart of a savage. But the heart of Nome was more savage than a wilderness.

A voice was shouting in me, straining at my throat. I wanted to leap onto my chair and yell at them that this was no girl to treat roughly, that if they had half an eye they could see for themselves that only some terrible need had forced her to do a thing like this.

Well, just then a Canuck shouted out—he was as lean as a greyhound and as soiled as a wolverine: "I'll start it off. I'll offer fifty dollars!"

There was a little, bald-headed man right in front of the Canuck. He turned, flashed his hand into the Canuck's face, and, in a moment, down went that fellow—*whack!*—against the floor.

"A good thing," said somebody near me. "Even if the girl's a rattlehead and foolish, she don't need to be insulted like that!"

The whole crowd seemed to agree with that remark, and the Canuck was helped toward the door at the end of fifty heavy boots, at least. He went out with a crash, and the door swung shut, letting in a good gulp of sweet cold air into the room.

Then I saw the ugly face, and the tall hat, and the bedraggled long hair of the Doctor—who owned The Joint—rising near the bar.

He said: "There ain't gunna be no ruction about this auctioning, boys. The first low crack that I hear, the gent that makes it gets the run, and the auction is off. They's gunna be order. You can make as much noise as you like, but it's gotta be decent noise. The lady'll be respected in The Joint, I say. Massey, are you back there?"

Every head flashed around. I did not see Massey, but the mention of that name was enough to insure law and order in any Nome crowd, no matter how big or how wild.

"Now, gents," said the announcer, "we'll listen to a real offer. How much am I bid?"

There was a general movement closer to the bar but, when the people came to a certain distance from it, they paused abruptly. Massey was in there, leaning on the back of a chair, and facing them, showing no disposition to budge. And near him was Doctor Borg, himself. They kept the people at a respectful distance.

And that poor girl, her eyes getting bigger and bluer every moment, looked desperately across the sea of rough faces, and gripped her hands suddenly together. But she did not climb down from the bar. Whatever was driving her, it kept her in her place there, on show before them all.

Someone I could not see offered fifteen hundred dollars. That was really the opening bid, and in two minutes the price was up to five thousand! It kept right on, but at this price the bidding settled down suddenly to two bidders.

One was a huge man—one of the biggest I ever saw. He must have been seven or eight inches over six feet, and he was built in proportion. He had a huge head, and a great, dark, inexpressive block of a face to crown the pile. His voice was like the rest of him, a deep, husky bass that boomed and echoed through that room in an amazing way.

He was the first man to go above five thousand.

The other bidder, who went to six at once, was an opposite type. He was young, clean-shaven, with a blond head of hair and a really handsome face.

The first glance at him made me pray that he would win out in the contest. He stood near the central stove, with his fine head thrown back a little, and his eyes never for an instant, until the end, wavered from the face of the girl.

I watched her, too, begin to look back at him. It was pretty plain to see where her preference lay, but that towering big man kept right on. The way he bid made me think that I could see the fashion he would have of marching through the snow, with long, regular, stride, never faltering, holding on like grim death.

They went up to eight thousand dollars in a very short time.

The bidding went like this:

"Eight thousand!" from "Blondy."

"And fifty," says the big man in his deep, sullen, bell-like voice.

"Eight thousand five hundred!"

"And fifty!"

"Nine thousand!" said the blond lad.

"And fifty," said the big man.

Blondy dropped his head and struck his hand across his face.

It was not a great deal. But it was plenty, in such a

crowd as that, to show that he had completely forgotten himself, and that his heart was all wrapped up in the girl who stood on the bar there.

"Going at nine thousand and fifty!" says the announcer. "Going at nine thousand and fifty!"

Blondy looked up again, and even through the smoke, and in the distance, I could see the desperation in his face.

As for the girl, actually she smiled at him, and such a wistful smile that it drew tears into my eyes.

"Nine thousand five hundred!" sings out Blondy, choking on the words a little.

You could see that it was about all he could afford, or beg, borrow, or steal, in this world.

And the crowd, which had been standing as still as so many mice when the cat is by, let go of themselves and their emotions in one wild whoop that must have budged the solid rafters overhead. I would have mortgaged ten years of my life, just then, to help Blondy win that contest.

"Redhead," forgetting the crowd and the eyes on her, made the smallest little gesture toward Blondy and smiled at him.

Yes, it is strange how that gesture and that smile strike back at me across the years, vividly, and sadly.

"Nine thousand five hundred offered," said the announcer. "Only nine thousand five hundred for the finest bit of auburn hair that I ever. . . ."

Massey turned his head and said quietly: "Stop that."

The room was so still that I could hear him perfectly.

The announcer, staggered in his speech, gulped as though he had seen a leveled gun, and then went on rather shakily: "Going at nine thousand five hundred dollars. . . ."

"And fifty!" said the giant.

There was a groan from the crowd. I groaned with them, as a matter of course.

The girl stood up straight and looked at Blondy as though the light of salvation were shining from him.

"Ten thousand dollars!" shouted Blondy wildly.

There was another yell that shook the walls of The Joint!

"And fifty!" said the imperturbable giant.

Blondy suddenly turned on his heel and waded through the crowd, head down, toward the door. He was finished, and I could see men slap him on the back and shoulders.

"Going at ten thousand and fifty," said the announcer. "Two times going at ten thousand and fifty. Going three times, and. . . ."

He took it for granted that the bidding was over. So did we all, when a voice cut in quietly—though with a growl in the tone: "Eleven thousand."

The giant's imperturbability was gone. He jerked around. So did every one, and we saw in the corner of the room a big man with an almost inhuman look of strength about his jaw and throat and his thick, smooth shoulders. He had a face like a wolf, heavy at the base of the jaws and rather sharp in front.

The giant, after one look, followed the example of Blondy, and waded for the door.

"By gravy!" said a man near me. "It's Calmont! He gets her!"

Chapter Seven
A Change of Mind

As surely as one bell stroke answers another, so that name of Calmont brought into my mind the thought of Massey. It was the same with every one in Nome, their suspended feud was so famous. I, jumping up on my chair, looked across the heads of the crowd and made out Massey again, near the bar. But he showed no interest in anything around him, except in keeping the place in order.

Calmont got the major part of the attention of the crowd. He had come well heeled for the thing that was to be done, and he plumped down a heavy canvas sack on the bar. It was plain that he either had known beforehand what was going to take place, or else at the beginning of proceedings he had slipped away home and come back with his treasure.

I think that gold went at something like seventeen dollars an ounce, and around thirty-three pounds were weighed out. Plenty was still left in the canvas sack to begin housekeeping, for that matter. Yes, I heard men say that Calmont had struck it quite rich and that, if he wanted to, he could have paid down ten times as much as this for the girl.

These things I heard close up, for I had made use of my small size and lack of thickness to slide through the jam like a snake, and so get to the bar, where the weighing out took place. Calmont stood by with an immobile face, the most formidable-looking man I ever have seen. If Massey seemed cold and hard, Calmont was plain mean, by the look of him, and my heart ached when I thought of the future that stretched ahead of that girl.

This may sound as though I were a bit dizzy about her, and, as a matter of fact, I was. Sixteen is the most sentimental age in the life of man, and the redhead was pretty enough to soften harder metal than my heart. The more hopeless I was about her, of course the more I mourned, like a great calf.

The girl had disappeared, and Calmont did not ask for her, but Doctor Borg was heard to say that she would be in his office the next morning before noon, and that a minister would be on hand to perform the wedding ceremony.

After this the majority of the crowd seeped away to the chairs and tables, but my excitement did not fade out so readily. I could not find Massey, in order to ask questions of him, so I began to do a little scouting on my own account.

When Borg took up the paid-in sack of gold, I saw that he went back to his office, and I waited below the horizon, so to speak, until I saw the door open a minute later, and the girl came out.

She went out through the deserted restaurant, casting guilty, secret looks about her.

The moment I spotted the way she was walking and acting, I knew that something was mighty wrong. It flashed into my mind that she might be a clever crook, who had played up the part of the innocent girl so as to raise a higher price. She was lugging a sack that was slung across her shoulder; but I would not have been surprised if that sack contained only a half of the money she had taken in. The rest was as likely as not to be resting in the cash drawer of Doctor Borg. He had not hesitated to take into camp men almost as formidable as Calmont, before this.

Yes, it looked to me very much like a put-up job, and in an instant I was after her down the aisle of the shadowy tables, for there was only a single lantern burning in the restaurant at that time of the evening.

She went out the side door onto the street. A blast of wind whistled past her and started me shuddering, but I hardly waited for her to get to any distance before I opened the door in my turn. I wanted desperately to follow her fortunes, on this night.

When I stepped outside, in my turn, there was nothing to be seen in that street except a whirl of snow dust that strode across the roofs like a phantom giant. But an instant later I had a sight of the girl as she hurried along straight into the eye of the wind, keeping close to the face of the buildings. I knew that it was she from her size and the weakness with which she kept her own against the gale. No man would have gone so slowly in such cold weather.

Out from a doorway stepped a man who looked to me about middle height, and nothing strange about him except, perhaps, the great swathing of furs that he wore. She gave him the sack from her shoulder, and I said to myself that this was the trick made clear—the money was for this fellow, and the two of them would get away together.

I halted. I despised her a good deal for the trick she had played, and myself for having been taken in by her good acting. But I did not have in mind to go back and tell that wolf-faced Calmont what I had seen.

Instead, I was about to turn and go on back to Massey's house, when I saw the fellow walk straight across the street and disappear down a lane. And the girl went on without him, alone!

When she turned at the next corner, I was close behind her, and behind her I kept as she turned and twisted. I could not make out the direction in which she was going, at first, but eventually I saw that she seemed to be drifting toward the edge of the town.

A little later, she was past the last house, and leaning well forward against the sweep of the wind.

That gale was strong enough even inside of the city, but where the flat plain let it go, it ran whooping and stamped in my face with both heels.

It was hard for me to keep my footing; the girl was fairly staggering, and as I peered through the storm until my eyes threatened to freeze in place, I wondered where on earth that girl could be headed for. Another explanation jumped into my mind, then. She had a confederate, out there in the storm who was to take her away from Nome, and Calmont, and her wretched bargain.

I was quite right. There was something waiting for her out there that she was very anxious to find, but it was not a man, though you might call it a confederate.

Pretty soon I lost sight of her, and this amazed me, because the surface of the snow was pretty flat, except for a low wind hummock here and there. I stumbled on, getting colder and colder with every step until it seemed that my vitals were being covered with frost. But I had food inside me now, and that's the fuel to turn the edge of a zero wind.

A moment later I had the solution of the mystery in my hands—literally. I nearly fell over the girl as she lay huddled in the snow. For half a second I thought that she had stumbled and knocked herself silly. Then the truth went home like a knife blade. She had lain down to die; death was the friend who was to take her away from Nome and Arnold Calmont.

It sickened me and it scared me, this knowledge. I had been pretty close to the same thing, that very day.

Now I caught her by the shoulder, but I did not have to pull her up. She leaped to her feet with a shriek and tried to tear herself away from me, but I kept a good grip on her.

She was wonderfully strong for a girl, but I managed to pull close to her, and all at once she cried out: "It's only the boy!"

And she stopped trying to tear herself away.

I shouted in her ear: "You've got to come back!"

"I'll never come a step," she said, "and you're not strong enough to carry me!"

It was true enough. If I tried to drag her back, she would be dead of the cold long before I got her there. Any way I looked at it, she had the game in her hands.

Then, cuffing my brain for a thought, I shouted again: "Come back with me and I'll promise that you won't have to go with Calmont!"

She caught hold of my coat and pulled at the lapels frantically.

"Do you mean it? You can't mean it! There's nothing that you could do! What could you do with Calmont?"

As she stammered and gasped these words at me, I saw that some small hope had jumped into her mind, even though she was arguing against me. I combed my mind. There was nothing in it. I simply shouted back that I would swear she would not have to go to Calmont if she would come back to Nome with me.

Well, it did not need much hope in a girl of that age to make her cling desperately to life again. In another instant, I had her started back toward the lights of the town, sparkling through frost, and the wind drove us along at a good clip, like small boats in a smooth sea.

We left the tundra edge and climbed down among the houses, and now with the edge of the gale turned by the high bank, we were able to talk more easily.

She had hold of my arm now, though I had been amazed by the speed with which she had walked. It had been plain that she was not one of those hothouse weaklings, but a free stepper, made with bone and muscle worthy of an athlete. Now, however, she seemed to lose her strength, and I could understand why. It was because she saw the houses of Nome closing around her, and to her they must have seemed like armed enemies.

She asked me again and again what my plan was. I had no plan. I could only mutter that everything would be all right and that she would soon see what I intended to do. Finally she stopped short.

She would not go another step, she said. She had been a fool to trust to the word of a mere boy. She felt that I meant well, but she knew that I could do nothing. She had been wrong to take the money from Calmont. But she had seen no other way! All that she knew now was that she would a thousand times rather die than fulfill her bargain.

"You've got to trust me," I said to her.

I looked wildly around me, but I could see nothing to

help, nothing that I knew, except the face of Massey's familiar house across the way. I pointed to it.

"If you'll go in there," I said, "I'll explain what we're going to do."

"I'll not go in," she said. "Heaven knows, I want to live, but I won't be trapped into living as Calmont's wife!"

"D'you think," I asked her, "that I followed you to bring you back to him?"

She hesitated. "No," she said at last, "I don't think you did."

"Come with me, then," I said. "We'll talk the thing out. There's no one in the shack. Come inside with me, and we'll have a chance to consider whether my plan's worth a cent. If it isn't, you'll be free to leave and do as you please."

Still she paused, staring at me as though she were trying to read the future in my face. Then she nodded.

"If it's only a shadow of a chance . . . ," she said.

And she went across the street with me to the house of Massey. I knew where the key was kept, and unlocking the door, we both stepped inside.

It was pitch-black, of course, and the darkness made her gasp, at which I freshened my grip on her arm.

"It's a trap . . . a trap!" she said, and pulled violently back.

"Be quiet!" I snarled at her, but I was too cold and tired to be polite, just then. "There's going to be no harm come to you here. Be quiet, and let me get a light going."

She got control of her nerves, after that. I closed the door and lighted the lantern in the corner, and put some wood into the stove and opened the dampers.

In a moment, the fire was hissing. The damp wood

crowded some smoke out through the cracks in the stove, and then heat began to come out to us. I kept myself busy at the stove. I dared not, for some reason, look at the girl.

Chapter Eight
To Solve the Problem

After a time the room began to warm up. That is to say, it got warm above the level of the top of the stove, but it was still icy toward the floor. It takes a long, long time and a red-hot stove to get a shack of any size warm down to the ground. However, when things were more comfortable, and I could no longer find an excuse for busying myself putting in more wood, or fooling about with the drafts, I had to turn about and face the girl at last.

She was looking straight at me. She had thrown back her heavy coat. Her hair hung down about her face, windblown and bedraggled. She was still as close to despair as a human being can come, but yet she was a long distance from being homely—or even plain looking. In fact, she was a lot prettier to my eye now than she had seemed in the barroom, and a thousand times more so than she had appeared this morning.

It was rather staggering to think that that morning I had seen her for the first time.

"Will you tell me your name?" I asked her.

"My name's Marjorie," she said.

"It's a nice name," I said.

"Thanks," she said, smiling a little at the absurdity of my compliment. But then, what were compliments to her?

After a moment, she said: "Joe, you might as well confess."

"What?" I said.

I was half-hearing her voice, and chiefly concerned with wondering why she had only given me one name. Of course, there were plenty of reasons. People who are ready to take their own lives are not apt to worry about names. She gave me one as a convenient handle in conversation; the second name might be Jones or Shakespeare. It made no difference, this far north, to a girl betrothed to that wolf of a Calmont.

"What?" I said, again.

"You've been bluffing," she said.

"I? Bluffing?"

"You have no more plan that a snowshoe rabbit."

"If we were a pair of snowshoe rabbits, we could hop back to God's country," I said.

She tipped back her head in a spasm of pain. She said not a word, but I knew that her very soul was melting and burning at the thought of the joy of being South, there in the land where we belonged.

"What part do you come from?" I asked her.

"Texas," she said.

"Texas!" I shouted. "Why, we're neighbors!"

"Are we?"

"Yes. I live in Arizona!"

She smiled faintly, but there was a wonderful lot of

sweetness in that girl's smile. Yet it made her seem a good deal older than I. I looked at her again, and felt that I had been pushed off to a distance. Then it occurred to me that Arizona, after all, is a fairish distance even from the butt of the panhandle of Texas.

"Well," she said, "I'd trade all the Northland for one acre of Arizona's most barren desert. But what's the good of talking about that? I want to know what plan you have, if you have any plan at all. Joe, don't try to beat about the bush and deceive me and waste time. You have a mighty good heart. I know that. But tell me quickly what's in your mind."

I stared at the walls to get an idea. The clothes of Massey and his rifle in the corner were the only answer that I saw.

So I said: "I think I know what will help you. I'm not dead sure. But it's a fairish chance, I guess. You're willing to wait here on a chance?"

"Yes. Tell me what it is."

"D'you know who this shack belongs to?"

"No. But somebody who's not a beggar, at least . . . and he keeps house neatly."

"Well, I'll go at it another way," I said, willing to use up a good many words for the simple reason that I was arguing myself into a certain frame of mind as I talked and listened to her, and answered back.

"Go any way you want about answering me, so long as you do that, Joe," said the girl.

Her voice was patient. Her eyes were literally burning with fear. Whenever the wind cuffed the door and rattled it on its hinges, her glance flashed away to it. Once, when it was violently shaken, she actually reached for the rifle in the corner nearest to her. That poor girl was already haunted, I could see.

"Well, you'll have to go back to Calmont for a minute," I told her. "Did he ever see you before tonight?"

"Yes."

"Here in Nome?"

"In Texas."

"He knew you there?"

"Yes."

This let in a flood of light of a different kind.

"He was a friend of yours there, Marjorie?"

"Friend?" she exclaimed, with a look and a voice of disgust. "Calmont, a friend?"

I thought I could see it. The pretty girl and the rough-looking man; he following, and she turning her head.

"Well," I said, "it's some of my business, too, because we ought to know just how set he'll be on having you back."

"Four years ago . . . oh, I was as tall as I am now, but I was a baby. Why, he would have married me then, if I had let him. Calmont! D'you know that I've seen him shoot down a man not ten feet from where I was standing?"

Her lips curled at the horror of the memory. It was plain that she hated this fellow as much as she feared him.

"It was a fair fight, I reckon?" I said.

"It's never a fair fight," she said, "when a gunfighter picks on a poor, ordinary puncher!"

That was true enough.

I said: "Look here, Marjorie, he really was pretty keen to marry you, and all that, and you wouldn't look at him."

"Of course I wouldn't. I'd rather . . . I'd rather look at a wolf."

"And then he happened to see you up here?"

"Yes. If I'd seen him there in the corner, at first, I never would have stood through the whole thing, because I might have known how it would turn out. He told me that day four years ago that he'd have me some time. And . . . and he's the kind who gets what he wants.''

She seemed to crumple, all at once, the strength going out of her, and her head dropped on her breast so far that I could see the round, tender nape of her neck.

Poor girl! I pitied her with all my heart.

''Well,'' I said, fumbling along the line which gradually had been straightening out before my mind's eye. ''Well, Marjorie, do you know any man in Nome who could stand up to Calmont?''

She raised her head, shook it instantly, and then added with a hasty afterthought: ''Massey, you mean?''

Their names were always so coupled together in story and legend and gossip, that nobody could mention one without the other popping into mind.

''Yes,'' I said, ''Massey is the man I mean.''

''Massey to help me? Is that your plan?'' she cried at me, half scornfully and half outraged.

''Why not?''

''Why not? Because Massey's a worse brute than Calmont. Because there's no heart in him at all. He looked at me there, tonight, as if I'd been an animal in a cage. Massey? He cares for nothing in the world . . . no woman, at least. He cares for nothing except the dog, and a chance to murder Calmont, one day!''

''Well,'' I said, ''perhaps that's it!''

''What!'' she exclaimed.

''Suppose Massey took your part and. . . .''

''He never would!''

''I say, just supposing he took your part, what would happen to Calmont? Why, Calmont would go pretty near crazy, wouldn't he?''

''Calmont? It would kill him, he'd be so mad.''

61

"And isn't that what Massey's waiting for?"

"Tell me what you mean, Joe!"

"Why, you know the story about them."

"Yes, that Doctor Borg made them swear never to attack one another again."

"And Massey will hang onto a promise. There's no doubt of that. So will Calmont . . . onto that promise. At least he will until something big and strong comes along to break it. But it would be easier to get Calmont to attack Massey than it would be to make Massey attack Calmont. That's what Massey is praying for, of course. That's why he's living here in Nome . . . not that he wants to be bouncer in a low dive, you see."

"He's living here to be near Calmont, you mean," said the girl, "in the hope that some day he can taunt Calmont into attacking him? Is that what you mean?"

"Yes," I said. "That's exactly what I mean!"

Well, up to that minute the thing had not been very clear in my mind. I had been fumbling along at it. First, I wanted to get her off the tundra and back to town. Then I took her into Massey's house because there was no other place where I could safely take her. And finally, out of our talk there, and the sight of Massey's clothes and guns, the whole idea grew up in my head.

It was a thing grim enough to chill my heart, I can tell you!

It chilled Marjorie, too. She stood up from the stool she had been sitting on and stared at me.

"Joe May," she said, "what sort of a young demon are you, after all?"

I managed to smile back at her, a little. "A friendly demon, I hope," I said.

"And I'm to try to get Massey to protect me, so that Calmont will attack Massey . . . and so . . . so that will be my way of paying back eleven thousand dollars to Calmont?''

"Did you give it all away?" I said.

She started. She came hastily over to me.

"What do you mean?" she said.

"I saw you give the sack to that fellow," I said.

She put up her hand like a child, to cover her face from my eyes. Then she moaned softly.

"Yes," she said. "It's all given away."

I stared hard at her, trying to make out what was what, and it seemed to me that it was not shame that I saw in her face, but sheer misery.

Just then the door opened, and Massey stepped in.

Chapter Nine
Massey Takes a Hand

With him, of course, was Alec, because Alec never was far away. The dog gave the girl a look, that was all. Then he came and licked my hand and sat down near the stove, wagging his tail across the floor and smiling at us in a way that only Alec could smile, as though he were asking what the next romp, or trick, or meal was going to be. That dog really seemed to enjoy a game more than he enjoyed food. If he had been a man, he would have been a poker player, sure enough.

Massey was as disagreeable as any man could be. Like Alec, he hardly noticed the girl, but he walked over and stood in front of me.

"What's this?" he said, and jerked his head toward Marjorie.

It was about the rudest action I ever saw on the part of any man. I could believe what the girl had said—that Massey cared for nothing but Alec, and a chance to kill Calmont, one day, if he had luck.

It appalled me to see the coldness of his eyes, and the anger in them, as well. Before I could answer, Marjorie was up and at the door. I darted after her, and Massey caught at my shoulder to hold me back.

I really think that he understood everything at a glance, even down to the suicide idea, and he was willing to let that girl go out and put an end to herself. But he missed his grasp at me, and I got to the door just in time.

"Let me through!" she muttered to me. "It's no use. I won't have it tried, anyway."

I held onto the door and shook my head.

"Massey," I said, "will you let me talk for half a minute?"

He glared at me. A vein stood out purple as an ink stain across his forehead, and for a moment I thought that he would throw me out that door and the girl after me.

"I knew that you'd spell trouble," was all he said, however; and he turned toward the stove, and started preparing to cook.

The girl motioned me away from the door. He had said enough to rouse up her pride, of course. It never needed so much rousing anyway. Not more than a wild horse needs a spur.

But I stuck to my place. With Massey turned away from me, closing his ears and hardening his heart against anything that I could say, my job was a hard one, but I would not give up.

I said: "Massey, she offered me money this morning, there at Tucker's place. She offered it because she saw that I was down and out."

"That's your business, not mine," said Massey, without turning his head.

And he began to scrape charred grease out of the bottom of a frying pan. There's hardly anything that makes so much and such a disagreeable noise as scraping a frying pan, as anyone can tell you, and I had to talk on over that accompaniment.

I tried again:

"When she left The Joint, tonight, I followed her."

"Because you're a simpleton, and a young simpleton, and that's the worst kind in the world!" he said.

Even this could not stop me.

"I saw her meet a man and give him what Calmont had given her."

"Yeah?" said Massey, and yawned.

"She went out from the town, and I followed her."

"A worse simpleton than before!" said Massey.

"Out on the tundra beyond town, she dropped in the snow and lay still!"

It was a high point. I expected that even Massey would be staggered by this, but I was wrong.

He merely said: "She knew you were close behind her, Joe!"

Imagine this, with the girl standing by to listen to it! Her head tipped back and her lips curled.

"Stand away from the door!" she ordered me, as proud as you please. "I want to get out!"

Of course she wanted to get out, and of course Massey wanted her to go; and I had to stand there, miserable and embarrassed, while I argued out that case and knew that I was losing it, every step of the way.

"I managed to get her to come back to town with me, because I said that I knew a way she could dodge Calmont," I said.

"If Calmont hears of that, he'll skin you alive," said Massey, "and I won't try to stop him."

"Calmont saw her four years ago in Texas and swore that he'd have her, some day," I said. "And he's tried to buy her tonight, and it's not right, Massey, and for Heaven's sake do something about it! You're able to. If you're not afraid of Calmont.''

I stormed through that last speech, and got to the final phrase before I really knew the meaning of the words that I was speaking. But this final touch made Massey turn around to me. A great shudder went through his body. He smiled at me in a way that I've never seen any other man smile, before or since.

''Calmont's wanted you for four years, has he?'' said Massey.

The first touch of hope leaped up in me, leaped through me. I could have shouted with excitement—but I held my breath, waiting for the girl to answer.

But she did not answer.

Of course she would not answer, after what he had said before. Her pride, and his pride, and I a foolish weakling between two strong souls, matured minds— well, I was ready to throw up my hands when Alec, as curious as a small child, came over and stood beside me and watched my face, and then as though sensing that all this trouble had to do with the girl, he went to her next and pulled at her sleeve to ask, ''Why?''

It was not a very great thing, considering what Alec was. But also keeping in mind that no one existed for him, really, except his master, it was a mystery, particularly at that moment.

Now, the girl had borne up very well through all that went before, but at this touch of dog sympathy, if one might call it that, she melted, and great sobs rose up and burst with a strange choked sound in her throat. She fairly ran to the door and tried to tear my hands away, so that she could go through and away into the night to hide herself and her emotion.

But I stood my ground and would not be budged by

any strength that was in her. She gasped something at me—a sort of prayer to let her go. Still I would not stir, and at last she collapsed against the wall and buried her face in the crook of her arm.

There she leaned, sobbing bitterly, while I, with my eyes dim with tears also, looked across at Massey. For this was my proof that she was real, and no silly, trifling sham. Such tearing, throat-filling sobs could not have come from any but a great heart, and of course he must see that!

See it? Why, he was looking at her with the coldest of sneers, the bitterest of smiles, as though he despised everything about her, and particularly this breakdown. I could not believe what my eyes saw. There was nothing but contempt in him for that girl, and her breaking heart.

Finally he came to the door and took Marjorie by the arm. "Come over here," he said.

"No!" she moaned back at him. "I want to get away. I don't want to stay."

He stepped back a little and I thought from his disgusted sneer that he would open the door and let her have her way about it, but he changed his mind, precariously, at the last moment. He freshened his hold on her and led her back to the stool near the fire. There he made her sit down, and a great burden, at the same moment, dropped from my shoulders.

"Look at me," said Massey.

She was so far gone with grief and shame and despair that she obeyed without thinking. Her head rolled back on her shoulders, and her miserable, tear-stained face, and the swollen eyes and trembling lips looked up at him.

You would have thought that even Massey would melt then. But not at all. He studied her like a jeweler looking for a flaw, and by the look of him I guessed that he saw plenty of these. Hard? Cast steel, tool steel, diamond points, were all extremely soft compared with this sneering fellow of a Massey!

Then I looked down to Alec, who stood at one side, wagging his tail and watching first the girl, then his master, as though he wanted to be told what he should do. Some hope came back to me as I looked at the dog.

"Can you talk?" said Massey.

She swabbed at her face with a handkerchief. "Yes," she said. "I can talk."

"If I'm to help you . . . ," said Massey.

"I don't want your help!" she said.

"You do!" I shouted at her, at the end of my patience, desperate at seeing her throw away this chance. "Of course you do. Massey's the only man in the world who can help you!"

Massey had stepped back, completely done, I thought. But the stuff in him was sterner than this. He came again, closer. He stood over her.

"Will you stop being foolish and childish?" said Massey. "Will you talk to me?"

She hesitated, trembling between her pride and her need, but finally she answered in a voice which she made suddenly calm: "Yes, I'll talk to you."

"Then tell me: Was that man to whom you gave the money . . . was that your husband?"

"No!" she said.

I could hardly tell whether she burst out with that in disgust or astonishment.

"He wasn't your husband," said Massey, beginning to pace up and down the floor. "He wasn't your husband. Your lover, then?"

She did not answer.

"Ah?" said Massey. "Fellow you were engaged to, eh?"

69

Still she did not speak, but set her teeth.

And Massey laughed. Or, rather, the brute that was in him laughed with his throat and mouth at that moment, a most ugly thing to hear, and still uglier to see.

Massey, hanging in mid-step to get the answer, took the silence as a sufficient response. He continued to laugh in that snarling way, and through the laughter he said: "Exactly like the simpletons! Let a good man rot, and sell themselves for the sake of some low sneak, some utter cur of a man!" He paused and then went on. "Whatever he was, he has your money. Calmont's, I ought to say. Now, what way do you see out of this? Death in the snow, apparently, was the only way. Touching, tragic idea! But hardly the thing to do. It answers nothing. It only beats Calmont out of money!"

He stretched out an arm at her, saying: "Calmont wanted you four years before?"

She managed to nod. She hated Massey, but he hypnotized her, as it were, into making answers.

"He wanted you four years ago. He bought you today, and paid high! That means that for four years you've never been out of his mind. By Heaven, it's for you that he's been saving his money like a miser, and working like a slave! You! You!"

Chapter Ten
Adventure Starts

This thought, or discovery, made him laugh louder than ever, until he was fairly whooping, but always with that ugly, wolfish snarl underlying the sound of his mirth. It was the most insulting thing that I ever saw or heard. You would have thought that he could not talk even to a brute beast as he was talking to this pretty youngster by the stove.

She watched him, all this time, with a strange fascination in her face. I think I understand what it was. This man was so extremely hard, so cruel, so biting, that he suddenly had ceased to be, in her eyes, a real human being. He was simply a freak. She listened to him and to his insults, as she might have listened to the raving of a lunatic. She had hardly more than a scientific interest, now, in the opinions of Hugh Massey.

Massey, resuming his talk, still was laughing to himself, but in a more subdued tone.

"It's for you that he starved himself, wore his hands

to the bone, treasured pennies, cheated friends, robbed
enemies, turned night into day. Always slaving away for
the beauty off there in the Southland. And you're the
one! You, selling yourself to him!''

He struck his hands together. He tipped back his head
and drew in his breath with a hiss.

''You that came up here, tagging on the trail of a lover
who didn't want you! You're the one that ruined Calmont! I've seen the day when he was the best friend,
the most honest man, the bravest standby, the straightest
bunkie in the world. He'd never fail you on a march.
Me . . . he's nursed me on the rim of gunfire and brought
me back to life. He's carried me on his back when I was
too weak to walk . . . carried and dragged me through
the snow. He's been my dog, and pulled me on a sled.
He's chewed willow slips, in order to give me the last
fish and flour. He's drunk hot water so that I could drink
tea. He's worked all day and sat up all night to take care
of me. You could search the world from the east to the
west and never find another like him. And then he turned
wrong! Well, I've always wondered why. It wasn't because of the dog. It's because woman is a disease that
sticks in the mind of a man and stays there, day and
night. He wasn't himself. It was woman that changed
him. . . .''

This began to frighten me. I've never heard anything
like the rapid, quiet, convinced way in which he talked—
to himself rather than to the girl. I began to understand
another thing, too—which was that he really had loved
Calmont, wolf though Calmont looked today.

''Whatever he was,'' snapped out Massey suddenly,
''I know what he is today. If you turned him crazy, we'll
turn him crazier still. To have you . . . to lose you . . . to
know that you're in my hands! Why, if he doesn't drop
dead with spite, like a snake that's bitten himself, he'll

come rushing out on our trail as fast as he can go! Let
him come! Let him come even with slow dogs, for he'll
find that we're not traveling too fast for him. Oh, he'll
be able to catch up with us!''

I watched the girl, and saw that she was straining her
ears to hear these last words, but that she had failed.

Then Massey came out of his frenzy and mastered
himself, as he was able to do, in a moment.

He hurried across to the girl and dropped a hand on
her shoulder. He said: ''I've been carrying on a strange
way. I want you to try to overlook that. From now on,
if you'll put yourself in my hands, you'll find that I'm
straight with you, kind to you, and that I've taken the
edge off my tongue. Will you try me?''

This put me in a strange mental mood.

The reason for this quick change in his attitude toward
her was sufficiently clear. He simply saw with clarity
that she would be the perfect bait with which he might
capture Calmont. The whole thing spread before me with
a wonderful simplicity. He would probably leave enough
clues for Calmont to follow, and then take to the road
and draw Calmont after him.

Certainly, Calmont would attack, if he got close
enough for the purpose, and such an attack was exactly
what Massey wanted.

That would free him from his oath and leave his hands
unburdened to defend himself. And of all that he wanted
between earth and sky, there was nothing so dear to him
as a chance to finish off with Calmont.

This was pretty much the way of the course his mind
was taking, as I guessed then, and as I saw proved later
on. I wondered if the girl would guess any of this. She
was watching Massey's changed face intently. Then she
said: ''I don't know what's going on in your mind. I

don't even know what sort of a plan you could have to help me.''

He said: ''It's a big job and a long one. We want to get out of the country where you made this bargain, and before so many witnesses. You want to get into Canada, say, as fast as possible. Now, there are several hundred miles of frozen sea, and rough overland, and the river ice of the Yukon to trek over before we could get to Forty Mile. But that's where I propose taking you. Will you go?''

She sat up as straight as a rod. Her eyes were so big that she looked as though she were trying to read in the dark. She was trying to read—the soul of Massey.

She looked across at me blankly, as the Herculean dimensions of this suggestion came home to her.

Clear across Alaska to the Canadian border!

''The boy'll go with us,'' put in Massey. ''He'll be our escort, as one might say. Our chaperon!''

He spoke very quietly. He laughed, and the laughter was like the subdued purring of a cat, as if he wanted his words to glide without a jar into her mind and become a part of her own thinking. Yes, he was almost tremulously eager, now, that she should accept his offer. She was straining to fathom its possibilities, but at last she broke out: ''There's no one else who could help me. I don't know what's in your mind. I don't know why you're willing to do such a thing for me. But I'll go! Several hundred miles? Oh, I'd go thousands and thousands!''

''Good!'' cried Massey.

He snapped his fingers. His face turned to ice again, and he began to pace up and down the room once more, with his eyes deep in thought. Finally he paused by the stove, and the dog, pausing with him, sat down to watch the wise human face above.

"Are you very strong?" he asked the girl.

"I'm mustang tough," she said, without a smile.

"You'll need all your toughness. What about clothes? Have you got an outfit for a march? Do you even know what such an outfit should be?"

"I know everything about it," she said. "I've every scrap that I need."

One could tell, by the way she said it, that she must have been turning the idea of a flight over in her mind, before this. Whatever were the strange circumstances connected with her stay in Nome, and whatever had made her sacrifice herself for the sake of eleven thousand dollars—I would have paid with pain to know the secret—she declared that she had every item ready for the longest sort of a trip. She had snowshoes and skis, both, and simply wanted to know which she should take along.

She said these things with a touch of eagerness, so that it was plain that she wanted to be in the fight of that long march as quickly as possible.

"You can get to your house," said Massey, "and make up your pack. It won't be too heavy for you to carry back here, I take it?"

She shook her head. She watched him almost like Alec, waiting for orders.

"Bring both the skis and the snowshoes. We can afford that much extra weight, and we'll save time on a long march if we have both. If you have a medicine chest, leave it behind you. We'll do enough hard work to keep us healthy on a long march. Now, hurry along."

She walked out of that house without a word and, as the door closed behind her, I turned and gaped like a fish at Massey. He went on in the same brisk way to me:

"Go down to the Penley store and get an outfit. Pick

out everything you need and get fitted. Do you know what's needed for a long trip?''

I said I did, but that I supposed the store would not be open at this time of the night. But he assured me that the place never closed now that the spring was coming on and the midnight was still bright. He said that Penley himself owed him an account, and that I was to get the best. He gave me a note, instructing the store to charge what I wanted against him.

"Massey," I said, "are you really going to do what you say? Are you really going to try to make the trip all the way to Forty Mile from Nome?"

He looked at me for a moment with an ugly lifting of his lip.

"I'm going to try to do it, and I'm going to succeed," he said. "We're going through to Forty Mile, and you'll be with us if you have the nerve to stick out the marching."

"I'll stick!" I said.

Stick with him? Why Nome to me was simply a cold cell, and any change had to be for the better.

I went trudging off to the store, and there I fitted myself out. I knew pretty much what I wanted and needed, and Penley himself made a good many suggestions. He asked if Massey himself were leaving Nome on a long trip, and was as keen as a ferret to find out. But I had sense enough to keep my mouth shut. I got well suited, though the boots were a little too big for me, and then I turned and slogged back to Massey's house on my brand new snowshoes, with the skis under my arm.

This trying and buying had taken a good deal of time and, when I got back to the house of Massey, I found there in the street a string of eight dogs in front of three sleds. I knew at once that this was the outfit for the long march, and I liked every angle of it. The Yukon hitch is the only one, and the little seven-foot sleds have every advantage on the trail when it comes to going over obstacles or winding among thick woods. They'll crawl along like a caterpillar and, if anything goes wrong with one of the three sleds, or it is overturned, it can be righted easily, whereas the bigger sleds have to be half unloaded before they can be handled.

I was surprised to find that there was quite a crowd turned out to watch the last of the loading of those sleds. Two men were busied at this job, the bystanders offering suggestions and admiring the dogs.

They were, in fact, as fine a lot as ever pulled in a harness in Alaska, I think. They were Mackenzie huskies, bred for size, and hand-picked, I suppose, out of thousands. The sled dog was the most powerful-looking brute I ever saw. Massey told me that he weighed exactly a hundred and seventy pounds, not when he was fat, but when he was in working flesh. In addition, there was a leader hardly five pounds lighter, and the average of that whole string of eight must have been over a hundred and fifty pounds.

One of the men tapped me on the shoulder.

"You're the kid Massey spoke about, are you?" he said. "Come along with me!"

I helped break out the runners, the steel having frozen into the snow during even the short halt and, as the word was given, the team leaned into the harness and we marched off down the street.

The long adventure had begun.

Chapter Eleven
Battle of the Dogs

I went on with those two strangers until we were outside of Nome, and then they turned around without a word and marched back to the town, while I trailed along after the moving sled, wondering what was to become of me and feeling mighty lonely in the bigness and the whiteness of the world around me.

Inside a hundred yards, however, two forms came around the edge of a snow hummock, with Alec the Great behind them. They swung in beside me, then Massey moved out in front on his snowshoes, and went ahead of the lead dog, to break trail. The girl and I came along behind, and we were fairly launched on our long, long journey.

For the first ten days, I think that I turned my head and looked at the horizon behind us at least a thousand times every twenty-four hours, but there was never a sign of pursuers. After that I almost forgot Calmont, and I began to have a feeling that Massey had undertaken this huge job merely for the sake of saving the girl. Yet I doubted that. I doubted it with all my might, and kept a certain suspicion always in mind.

Dreary, heart-breaking weeks of labor opened before us and dragged away behind. A more uneventful trip no one could possibly imagine in the beginning; but what kept my nerves taut was a certain forward look in the eyes of Massey, as though he were leaning his shoulders against a high wind of chance that was sure to promise trouble before the end. In the meantime, the breaking into that labor was enough to occupy our attention, you can be sure.

One had to grow used to the muscle strain of snow-shoes and skis—each requiring a different set. And before we had been going a week, we all could bless the wisdom of Massey in making us take along both kinds of footgear.

The load was almost entirely food for man and dog, and it was very heavy. I think there was close to three quarters of a ton for the eight dogs to pull, and they snaked it along slowly. I imagine that we hardly covered more than twenty miles a day at the beginning, and those twenty miles were enough for me and for the girl. She was what she had called herself, however—mustang tough. And she worked into marching condition very quickly. My own misery in Nome had burned the fat off me. It was simply a question of working up the necessary muscle, and muscles grow nowhere so fast as they do on a snow trail.

As the dogs grew hardened to their work, as the girl and I became more tough and proficient with the snow-shoes and skis, we made better and better time. Besides, the load of food was, of course, slowly diminishing.

Several times we ran into storms that stopped us for long hours. But on the whole, we marched along very steadily, clicking off a good average. At night we camped, put up the two little tents, got the traveling stove going, and cooked bacon, flapjacks, and tea. We had some pemmican, too, put up Indian style. At first I thought that that was the worst food I ever tasted, but it seemed to get better from day to day, and within a fortnight, it was a delicacy. Pound for pound, I doubt if a finer article of food existed—such nourishment and taste in such compass.

The picking of the trail was entirely in the hands of Massey. He had three charts, done roughly in ink on thick pieces of paper, and over these charts he used to brood almost every night, sitting for a time by the fire. Then he and I went to the cold tent and left the warm one for the girl.

We were a silent trio.

Massey never was a chatterer, and the girl had too great an anxiety on her shoulders to do a great deal of talking. After a while we had our jaws locked and our teeth set against speech, as though the escape of a word would be the wastage of a vital spark.

I can remember almost every word that was said during the first part of the trip. Almost all of these were spoken by Massey to Alec the Great. For Alec was being taught how to answer the words of command and all the art of leading a string of dogs, which was something he already knew pretty well. He simply had to have the fine points at the tips of his toes, so to speak. So, each day, he was put in on extra traces ahead of the big gray leader.

That dog went almost mad with indignation. He had to be muzzled to keep him from jumping on Alec and breaking his back for him; and he struggled so frantically to get at Alec that the young dog could be left in harness for only an hour or so at a stretch. He picked up the sledding art with wonderful speed, however.

One day, during a halt, Massey stood with his feet spread, snapping the long lash of the dog whip at Alec, who was free from harness at that time. The big, limber fellow enjoyed that game enormously. According as the lash flicked out at him with a down cut, or a slash to either side, he winced back, dropped flat so that the whip sang over him, or popped into the air so that it slid beneath him. He loved the dodging game, and there was enough wolf blood in him to give him a special talent for it. Considering his size, I never saw a dog who compared with Alec the Great for speed of foot. He not only had a natural talent, but he had been trained since puppyhood by Massey in the art of balance. I could believe what I had heard, that he could even walk a tightrope.

Said Massey, as he vainly cut and slashed at that big shadow: "I don't think there's a dog in Alaska that could put a tooth in Alec."

"Well," I said, "you wouldn't risk a ten-thousand-dollar brain on a fight with a two-hundred-dollar husky, would you?"

He shrugged his shoulders.

"No team follows well a leader that it doesn't fear," he said. "That gray brute, yonder, that Misty . . . he can have it out with Alec when we camp, tonight."

I thought that he could not mean it, but when the end of the march came that day, he took Misty out of the traces, allowed him a couple of hours for resting, and then got Alec out of the tent, where he was sleeping at our feet.

Those sled dogs all hated Alec with a fury, because he was the manhandled pet of the party. But they had learned, by dint of whip strokes and club whacks as well, that it paid to leave the favorite alone. However, this evening Massey said something to Misty, and pushed Alec at the great leader.

That was enough of an invitation. Misty rushed like an arrow off the string. Alec dodged with such ease that he had to turn his head toward his master and ask, with his eyes, what this proceeding might mean, and why protection had been withdrawn from him. But Massey simply turned his back.

It must have been a frightful moment for Alec. Every young dog is keenly aware that it has not yet come to its eventual, hardened strength, and it willingly shows the white feather. As Misty charged, Alec, his tail between his legs, yipped for help, and tried to get between Massey's legs. He was promptly kicked away, and from that instant he seemed to guess that he was fighting for his life.

It was a grand fight, too, while it lasted. Misty was pretty well tired out by his long labors of the day, but at the same time there was enough energy left in him to beat and eat two or three ordinary dogs. There were no two dogs in the outfit, including the huge wheeler, who dared to take on Misty in battle. However, poor young Alec had to fight as well as he could, or else die. So it must have seemed to him.

He could not even take refuge in flight. He knew that if he turned tail and ran for it, the seven brutes who stood around in hostility with the fur rising along their backs would cut loose and be after him in no time at all. He had to stand his ground, or else be eaten by the pack. So he stood his ground.

For the first couple of minutes, I held my breath, expecting that Alec would go down under those charges in no time, and perhaps have his throat torn by the knife stroke of Misty's teeth. Then I began to breathe more easily, for I saw that Alec was dodging those battle strokes as easily as a dead leaf in the air whirls from a beating hand.

His own courage rose. His tail came out from between his legs. In another instant, he gave Misty a nip as the big fellow went by like an express train; and on the next charge he followed the nip with a slash that split hide over Misty's left shoulder.

Misty, furious, panting, half blind, I suppose, with rage and astonishment, stopped charging for a moment, and on braced legs waited for further developments. Young Alec, it appeared, was not only an adept at battle, but, above all, he knew how to deliver an insult in dog gesture. He turned a little away from Misty and licked up a bit of snow, with his side presented to the leader.

It was too much for the latter. He went in with a silent fury, and hit the air again. He whirled, skidding in the soft surface snow which already had been reduced to powder by the trampling. As he straggled, young Alec got him. He had saved his stroke until he saw an opening as wide as a barn door. Now he flashed in, and with a good solid thump of his shoulder he knocked Misty sprawling on his back. Alec did not stand back and let the other fellow get up. There was no standing on rule about Alec. He simply hopped on Misty and clamped the safest of holds on him. I mean, he caught him under the jaws and began to work his grip in toward the life.

Misty could lie and kick, but that was all. The fight was over, and Massey, with a single word, made Alec jump back from his enemy.

Misty lay a moment on his side, with lolling tongue, while Alec stood stiff and high above him, daring him so much as to whisper a discourtesy. Misty did not dare. He had had enough. The rest of the dogs had had enough to fill their eyes, also. They lay down in the snow and licked their forefeet thoughtfully, and poor Misty finally got up and staggered away to get distance between him and this young terror of a man-trained fencer.

Well, it was on the whole a very neat exhibition.

"I never saw anything like it," I gasped to Marjorie.

Then I saw that her eyes were fixed on Massey's face, and with such a deep attention that I knew, suddenly, that all during the dog fight she had been watching the master, not Alec. I stared at Massey in turn, to discover what had fascinated her; and it seemed to me that I saw nothing in his eyes and faintly smiling mouth but the remnants of what had been, a few seconds before, a brutal delight. If Marjorie had a pale look and failed to answer my remark, I did not wonder. It's all very well to take pleasure in a good fight but, after all, there's a certain point past which one should not go, and Massey had gone past that point.

It was the very morning following this that I said suddenly to him: "Massey, I don't think that Calmont is going to show up after all."

He turned sharply about on me, but I had not surprised him into making an answer. He simply smiled, but his eyes brightened and narrowed in the same brutal satisfaction which I had seen in his face during the dogfight of the evening before.

No matter how long delayed it might be, I knew now that he was confident that he would meet Calmont before Forty Mile.

Chapter Twelve
Bad Luck on the Job

We traveled out of the skirts of winter into the warmth of spring, for it was spring when we hit the Yukon, and a strange, wonderful sight it was to me, with its banks streaked and darkened by brush and little trees, and the frozen surface of a macadam road. What made this bulge I don't know, unless it were the pressure of water rising in the bed of the stream. The sides of the ice sheet were frozen fast to the banks, and the big strong sheet of ice gave in the center a surprising lot without breaking. You would not think that there could be so much elasticity in such hard, brittle stuff. To increase the likeness to a road, there was water running down the shore on either side. This water was from the melting of the surface ice itself, and the thawing along the banks, and little rivulets unlocked by the sun long before the great main stream was free from the ice. The swift stream on each side of the ice sheet made this long, winding, shining white street like a part of a great municipality which floods the gutters for the sake of cleanliness. In what sort of a city would the great Yukon be a street!

Well, it seemed like a street to us, after the rough going we had had—the up-hill and down-dale struggling. We had dropped the third sled the day before, and with only two to pull, and with the team in very good fettle, we went fairly humming up the face of the ice. Massey said that the river might break up at almost any time, and that we had better make good time while we could, so we stretched out those days long and fast. Once again he gave me the impression not of a man who wanted to linger so that he might be overtaken, but of a fellow in desperate haste to meet someone ahead of him. But I was wrong.

At any rate, we went along at a smart clip, getting foot wise on the ice, with Alec spending most of his time in the lead traces. He was not very good at pulling—he was too intelligent to do much work when it was not a crying necessity—but he knew exactly where to find the best going; sometimes on the crest, and sometimes down the side of the easy curve of the river face, and sometimes weaving cunningly back and forth to avoid the roughnesses and the riffles in the surface ice. Other leaders were apt to put their heads down for pulling, but Alec kept his head high. He let the others do the hard slogging. He did the seeing and the thinking for the rest. And by this time they were taking much more kindly to him. It is my conviction that a dog team knows and respects the brains of its leader even more than his superiority in tooth work. Those eight big, strong, experienced huskies learned to look up to young Alec like children to a schoolmaster, and a very odd sight it was to see him wander about among them when we camped, lording it over them to the queen's taste.

Of course, we went ashore to camp every halting

stage. It was wet work getting to land across the deep, swift currents in the gutters; but we hardly minded that wetting because, once on shore, there was sure to be an ample supply of wood, and we could dry out in front of roaring fires, with the dogs lying about outside and the firelight reflecting copper green in their steady eyes.

One day, we began to feel a strange sense of life in the ice and, beyond the feeling, there were the oddest sounds that I ever heard. Massey said that it was a sign the ice would break at almost any time. There was no real danger, I suppose, because the roar of the breaking above or below us was reasonably sure to give us plenty of warning, yet I could not help a definite sense of fear, as though the great ice sheet over which we traveled might explode beneath our feet. We passed another dog team, that day, three dogs and two men, with two sleds. They were slogging along head down, so desperately bent on making mileage before the break-up of the ice that they paid little attention to us, and we went by them like something in a dream. I shall never forget, however, the strained, set expression in their faces. Ten miles out there on the ice could be covered without much more difficulty than one mile in the soft snow along the banks of the stream. They were trying to stretch out their easy mileage, and I didn't blame them. We were doing the same thing, but we traveled like a flock of birds compared with the slogging of those poor freighters.

One or two mornings after that we sighted Calmont's outfit behind us.

We had broken camp and repacked the sleds when I ran back to the top bank to hunt for a sheath knife which I had left behind. I got it on the tent site and came back through the brush to the verge of the bluff. Then I saw, far to the right and around a great arc of the curving river, an outfit of dogs and three men. There were eight dogs, just as we had in our regular outfit of workers, and there were three humans, just as in our string.

The minute I saw it, a sense of danger jumped up in my throat and half choked me. That was not exactly strange. We were making a good, early start, and something special must have been in the minds of those three travelers back there on the ice. Of course, it might be that they were simply trying to make good mileage before the break-up came. I said to myself that that must be it, but I called down to Massey what I had spotted.

He had a small pair of field glasses, an extra weight which I always wondered at his carrying. Now he pulled these glasses out and tossed them up to me. Imagine such a thing! He would risk throwing them about in this way after he had carried them so many hundreds of miles. Suppose they had fallen and the lens had been broken; he simply would have shrugged his shoulders, I know. He was that way. He had a strange belief that fate was directly concerned in everything that happened to a man.

Well, I got those glasses to my eyes and focused them on the outfit. I could not make out faces, at that great distance, but I thought I could tell that, compared with the size of the sleds, the dogs and men were big.

"What's the leader like?" asked Massey.

Just then I got the glasses to a perfect focus, and into the round, steady field walked the dog team in the distance. I could make them out with extraordinary clarity.

"A black dog with white on him . . . a white vest," I said.

I lowered the glasses, blinking from the eye strain, and I saw on the face of Massey a look of wild joy. I did not need to ask questions, and neither did the girl. She took one look at that frightful, leering smile and knew that it meant murder.

Yes, actual murder in the eyes of the law. If Calmont had come up with us, and had brought men along to help, we could be sure that one of them would be wearing a deputy's badge. Massey would be resisting arrest. On what charge? Hardly on that of abducting a woman who had been bought like a horse or a dog by another man. No, not on that charge would they have their warrant made out, but on any one of a hundred little minor charges. I thought that I could see the story and the end of it in a blinding flash and roar of guns—and if Calmont and both his men went down, then Massey would be a hunted, hounded manslayer the rest of his days.

What did Massey care for that? His hatred of Calmont was such a perfect and compelling thing, that death itself was not too high a price to pay, if only he could send Calmont to eternity before him. He paid no attention to us. He simply pulled out his rifle and set about loading it. Marjorie, at this, ran up to him and grabbed the gun by the stock and the barrel. She had no words to say, but the desperation and the horror got up to such a high pressure that she cried out in a stifled little screech. She looked as a dumb person might. I never saw such a dreadful expression as she wore, standing there before Massey and realizing that nothing she could say would have the least effect in altering that brute of a man.

She did not persist. She did not try to argue but, realizing at once that she was helpless, she loosed her grip on the gun and turned to run down the face of the river ice. I could see her idea, of course. She was desperate enough to go back and throw herself into the hands of Calmont if, in that manner, she could stop the fight between the two men.

She got hardly six steps away when Massey overtook her, and picked her up like a baby in his strong arms. At that, she gave up. He sat her down on the rear sled and she took her head between her hands and began to sob in the same awful way that I had overheard that morning so long ago in Nome.

In the meantime, Massey looked up to the bank and was, I suppose, planning the way in which he would begin this action. He kept nursing the rifle in his hands in an odd way. I remember that it was very bright sunshine, that morning, with hardly any mist in the air, and the reflection from the ice threw a bright glow on the under part of his face. He was still smiling, and horribly at ease, and even more horribly sure of himself. This, as I write it down, does not seem very exciting, but to stand elbow to elbow with murder is a frightful thing.

However, there was no doubt in my mind as to what I should do in this business. Massey was my partner, and I had to stand by him no matter what crime he was committing. At least, that was my reasoning at the age of sixteen. Besides the rifle, we had a good new Colt revolver. I got this out, loaded it and, when Massey started down the river edge, I went along with him.

He jerked his head over his shoulder and told me to go back. I felt as though there were no breath left in my lungs, and my knees were weak as old springs, but I kept along after him. He stopped, turned a little, and gave me a long, hard, calculating look. Then he showed me his back without another word and marched on.

A rabbit jumped in the brush above us, and he whirled to shoot. We were so close to the bank, and the bluff itself was so high, that there was no danger of the report echoing across the ice and down the river to Calmont and his men. So Massey decided to give himself a little practice, I suppose, and tried a snapshot at that rabbit. It made the old snowshoe jump as high as a man's head. As it landed, Massey had thrown out the old shell and was ready to fire again. He pulled the trigger. There was not the true rifle report—like a hammer face clanging against a wall of steel—but a puffing, dull sound. I saw fire and black smoke leap from the breech of the rifle into Massey's face and, dropping the gun into the running water of the gutter, he staggered back, his hands pressed against his face.

I followed him. There was such an overmastering horror in my mind that I lost my fear of this man and, catching him by the wrists, I jerked his arms down so that I could see what had happened.

There was a black smudge straight across his eyes, almost like a mask. This meant apparent ruin to us all, but I could not think of Marjorie and myself, just then. All I could do was to stare at the downfall of my friend, and the only words that came out of my mouth were a groaning: "Oh, Massey, Massey!" two or three times over.

Massey was as calm as a drill sergeant on parade. The burning of the powder, which must have been an exquisite agony, made the tears run down his cheeks; but his voice was perfectly steady when he said to me: "Aye, sonny. Bad luck is on the job today. I thought we might catch it off its beat. Give me the revolver, will you?"

I stretched it out. He reached, fumbling in the darkness of his sight, and this glimpse of his helplessness choked me with pity. It did not occur to me to question what use he could make of a revolver, now that his vision was lost, and I was about to put it into his wandering hands when Marjorie came up like a tiger and tore the gun away from me.

She had understood!

Chapter Thirteen
Blind Leaders

If the girl and I were confounded and upset, that was only natural. The strange thing was to see the way Alec carried on. You would have said that he knew what had happened. He ran whining to his master and stood up with his big paws against the breast of Massey and his head almost as high as the man's.

Massey took the big pup in a hug, then made him drop down.

"Take Alec, Joe," he commanded me, as steady as ever. "He'll obey you. You're the one person that he gives a rap about, outside of me. You saved his hide for him once, and the day'll come when he'll do as much for you. Treat him as if he were your child. Reason with him. But always be firm. Make a game out of him and he'll repay you with an ocean of fun. Now, take Alec and tie him behind the rear sled. He may cut up for a time, but he'll soon follow along. Tie him with that length of chain. And send the sled straight up the river.

Keep the dogs working. They'll stay ahead of Calmont's gang, I think. Besides, I may decide to check them here for a time.''

"How will you check them?" asked Marjorie.

"By getting up the bank here after they're in sight. They ought to be in view now."

They were. It was not a bad idea, if he wished to throw himself away. If they saw a man climb from the river to the bank and go into the brush, of course they would know that it was Massey, for they would be able to identify our outfit by the appearance of white-bodied Alec. And they would not dare to pass the place where Massey was hidden without scouting with painful care for him. That would give us hours of a vital advantage. I could see the value of this plan, but I could not make up my mind to throwing Massey away. I looked at the girl, and she at Massey.

"We're not leaving you, Hugh," she said.

"What!" he roared out, as if he were furious. "You're crazy! What could you do with a blind bat like me? Get on up the river. Alec, come here and say good-bye to me. . . ."

"If you're staying here, I'm staying," said the girl. "If you stay, I'll be here and stop the murder!"

"If you go to Calmont, you're not worth the saving!" he cried.

But he turned a little from side to side, apparently pretty much disturbed by this threat.

"Get her away from here!" he said to me. "Joe, take the girl and tie her on the rear sled, if you can't do it any other way. . . ."

"I'm staying here with her, too," I said, "if you're waiting, Hugh. They're coming up pretty fast, and it'll soon be over for us. It'll be a good day for Calmont when he gets Marjorie and Alec, and takes your life. It'll be about the best day in his life!''

When Massey heard all those things piled up on his attention, he threw his arms over his head with a groan, and the look of him was like some one strangling in flames.

"All right," he said. "I'll go on with you if I can. You're throwing yourselves away for my sake. Danged little I care for that, except that you'd fall to Calmont after me!"

We hardly cared what reasons influenced him. All that mattered was that we finally had him up there with the sleds, and his hand leaning on the gee pole. Then we strung out the dogs and started up the face of the ice.

But this time, the Calmont outfit or what we took to be his gang, had come up to within about a half mile of us, and immediately after we ran into a land mist that blotted out everything within two or three hundred yards, so that we could not tell whether we were gaining or losing.

Perhaps I should have called that a river mist, because I suppose that it was raised from the thawing ice and the melting of the frozen banks. At any rate, it was as white as smoke, with the sun path as a streak of blinding yellow across the frozen face of the river. This is the sort of traveling—as one strains the sight through the fog—that gives snow blindness. Both Marjorie and I were shaking our heads and rubbing our eyes, from time to time.

If we wanted to make proper time, we saw quickly that it could not do to have poor Massey on the gee pole. The reason was that he could not see his footing, of course, and he was continually stumbling over irregularities, which inevitably threw his weight against the pole and made the sled swerve. Marjorie and I talked about him with mere glances at one another, while we studied the situation. She got a strip of bandage and a bit of salve from her pack and, without halting the march for a second, she tied this about his wounds. One moment it made him look to me like a grown man playing blind-man's bluff. The next moment, I was again realizing that the goal in this peculiar game was life or death.

From the first, it looked a perfectly helpless job that we had undertaken. Even supposing that Marjorie and I had an excellent string of dogs—as good as cleverness and money could collect—still it would have been practically impossible for us to get away from the expert and hardened dog-punchers who were following up that river trail. But burdened with the practically helpless bulk of Massey, the little hope that we might have had was taken away from us.

Eventually, Marjorie had a good idea, and we acted on it. We tied a lead to Alec's harness, and gave the end of the strap to Massey. After that, he went along much more comfortably. Alec pulled like a Trojan, until his master made him slack up. Then they went along very easily, because the dog, going over rough or smooth, or turning from one side to the other to avoid rough patches, was sure to give some signal of the change in direction to his master at the end of the lead line. Besides, Massey was an old-timer on ice, and knew almost instinctively how to handle himself. He had eyes in his feet, and he grew rapidly better and better at the marching game.

With occasional pauses, we slogged on through that day until the late afternoon, when the fog lifted by magic and we could see for miles up and down the bare face of the river.

There was no sign of Calmont's train.

All that day we had been going on with the blind dread tapping us between the shoulder blades and making me, at least, feel pretty sick. And when that blanket of white was peeled off from the face of the Yukon, I could have cried, I could have sung, I could have danced, even on my weary legs.

I ran up and clapped Massey on his shoulder—padded with rubbery muscle like a panther's arm—and told him that we had distanced Calmont.

He listened to me and nodded. "You won't distance Calmont," he said. "You may drop him below the skyline, now and then, but you haven't distanced Calmont as long as he is on the same planet with you."

You cannot imagine the calmness and the surety with which he said this. Marjorie and I knew that he understood Calmont perfectly, having been such friends with him long ago. We had to take what Massey said for gospel, or just about, and the ecstasy faded out of us instantly.

We kept slogging on, therefore, getting more valuable miles behind us, until Massey advised that we halt and make camp, which he said was what Calmont was probably doing. He pointed out that one very punishing march was likely to dry up our marching power for the next day—dog and man. There was sense in this. My own legs were numb to the hips, and how Marjorie managed to keep up, I never could tell. Her face was pinched with effort, but she had not said a word, and she never asked for a single halt.

We had reached a point where the ice along the bank had broken loose from the ground, so that the deep and swiftly running gutter water did not have to be crossed. It was easy to get up the bank into good camping ground and there, sure enough, we saw the smoke of a fire down the river behind us, a couple of miles away, the thin film rising through the sunshine, for the sun was above the horizon. At midnight, in this season, the sky is bright.

The sight of the camp fire was only a partial consolation. For all that we knew, it might be a bluff under the cover of which they would sneak up behind us; but Massey, always calm, pointed out that this was a game in which we all would have to take a gamester's chances.

We built our own fire as small and of as dry wood as possible. In this way, little or no smoke rose, except for a puff or two at the beginning, and we cooked the usual meal for ourselves and for the dogs.

Marjorie did her share of the work, her lips still locked over her fatigue. When she had eaten, forcing down the food, she dropped into her sleeping bag and was instantly gone from us.

I was dead enough to want to do the same thing. But I stared across at the bandaged face of Massey and wondered what thoughts were going the rounds in his brain.

I got out his sleeping bag, and he slid into it. Still I waited for a moment beside him, patting Alec's head and looking down at the set mouth and the iron-hard jaw of my friend.

"Hugh," I said, "it might be that during the night you'd be tempted to get up and walk away from us. I want you to promise me that you won't."

"Go to sleep," he said, "and don't bother me."

"If you won't promise," I said, "I'll have to tie myself to you and then, in case of a surprise, we'll most certainly be goners."

His lips twitched a bit. Then he groaned: "All right. Have it your own way."

I took his hand. "Will you shake on that, Hugh?" I said.

He gritted his teeth, then gave my hand a convulsive grip and turned on his side. It was a great victory for me and a great load off my mind, for I knew that his word of honor was as strong as his punch. He was famous for it.

Then, like a stone dropped from a height, I sank into such a sleep as very few men ever have. No dream could come near me through the thick wall of my utter weariness.

Yet I waked suddenly several hours later and sat up with my heart beating to a wild tune. I thought at first that one of the dogs must have moved, but there was nothing to be seen or heard around us in the ragged woods. Alec got up like a ghost from beside his master and came over to look into my face with his bright, wise eyes.

Outside the tent, the night air was cold, for although the days were bright and warm, the night temperature was always below freezing. The dogs were breathing white as they slept. Rimings of frost appeared on all the twigs and branches around us; the steam of our cookery, I suppose, having condensed there.

I squinted through the brush toward the point at which we had seen the campfire smoke at the end of the day's march, but of course there was no trace of it now. I wondered what they were doing. Still sleeping soundly, or just turning out and getting ready for the day's struggle. Alec, walking beside me, turned his head and looked up into my face. He seemed to me to be asking something, and perhaps it was this questioning attitude of his that made me feel that I must do something for my party—and the next instant the perilous idea of what it should be was in my mind.

Chapter Fourteen
Up and Stirring

I determined that I would make a solitary march to the camp of the enemies and do what I could to embarrass them in their progress for that day. The idea frightened me cold, but there is a peculiar logic in despair, and I knew that if something were not done, they would most certainly capture us.

Then what?

Massey would probably be butchered before our eyes. My remembrance of the wolfish face of Calmont was enough to assure me of that. And then the girl would go to Calmont, and Alec as well—and as for me? Well, dead boys as well as dead men tell no tales.

However, I was set on going down there and trying my chances.

I did so, though it is hard for me to believe that I could have found the courage for such an effort. I had been a boy up to that moment, but standing there in the arctic night among the frozen willows I became a man in a brief and burning moment of torment. For the definition of manhood, I take it, is that quality which enables people to strike out for themselves, and for those who are near and dear to them.

Well, Marjorie and Hugh Massey were near and dear to me. For her I had an oddly combined feeling of tenderness, pity, and respect. She was so brave and quiet, so gentle and strong, that I loved her with something more than the usual flabby sentimentality of a boy. As for Massey, now that he was blinded and his strength useless to him or to us, I seemed to see him more clearly than ever before. I could not deny that there was a wide strain of brutality in him and that he was capable of great cruelty; but I began to feel that all these bad traits were due to the long-continued hatred which existed between him and Calmont. Hatred is a definite poison in the blood and in the brain. It may sharpen the wits; it may give one the strength of ten; but the wit and the strength of hatred is more than half madness. I was able to see Massey now as one who had long been sick in the brain.

He appeared to me, also, with a new and special dignity, for it did actually seem to me that it was an act of Providence that had blinded him when he was on the verge of a triple killing—into which I would have been dragged almost as a matter of course, and in the course of which he might have gone down himself.

Well, that was behind us. The power was gone from poor Massey, and I saw a ruined life stretching ahead of him.

This, with a curious power, was what drove me on this still, bright night.

I had a good hunting knife, sharp as a razor. That was to be my tool. I thought of taking the revolver with me, but I remembered that I was not much good with that weapon and that, if it came to a shooting scrape, I would have no chance against such a fellow as Calmont, even if there were not two others to support him.

So I started off down the ice of the river, with Alec alongside. Now and then he halted, as though tempted to go back to his master. But, after all, his master was safely sleeping, and adventure lay in the white world of the outdoors. So Alec faithfully went along with me, and I was wonderfully glad to have him.

I could have gone through the woods, but there was a cutting wind that began to blow out of the east, and the bluff of the river gave me a good shelter against it.

It was fully two miles that I traveled before I found the place where the sleds had turned in to the bank. I went up the trail which they had left slanting up the bank, and I was grateful to the rising force and the whistle of that wind because it made enough of a noise to drown any sounds that I made in approaching.

I stuck my head up over the top of the bluff as carefully as any soldier looking out of a trench with the enemy twenty yards away. Of course there would be a guard, with such an enemy as Massey within twenty miles, to say nothing of two.

And I was right. There sat the guard outside the tent, mending some dog harness with clumsy, mittened hands. I watched him with a sinking heart.

It was not Calmont, but it was a fellow who looked almost as formidable, with a great pair of shoulders and a foolish-looking little head stuck down in the middle of them. I saw the frost on his whiskers and heard him snort a little at the cold, now and then. He seemed a patient sort of a fellow, sitting there at his awl work, pulling the leather lacings through with infinite pains. My heart sank, I say, when I saw him, but I hoped that I would have a chance to give him infinitely more repair work before the morning came.

I think I lay there shuddering with excitement and cold for half an hour. Every minute frightened me more, because it was drawing closer to the time when they would get up and stir about in preparation for their day's march.

Circle City, according to the calculations of Massey, lay about two days' march away. We never could get there ahead of the pursuit unless I put a spoke in their wheel, so to speak. So I gritted my teeth and prayed for my chance.

It was there in my sight, but beyond my power, for a moment, to reach. The guard had been reviewing all the dog harness, it seemed, for a big pile of it was beside him.

After a time, the cold got too much for him, and he got up and stuck his head inside the flap of the tent. He withdrew again and, cursing softly beneath his breath, he walked through the willows straight toward the spot where I lay.

This I had not expected. Why, I cannot say. Of course, it was a logical thing for him to go to the edge of the bluff and look up the white face of the river ice, now and again, but that had not occurred to me, and now I dared not move. I had to lie there like a wretched log while this fellow strode up to within five feet of the spot where I lay on the edge of the bluff, with Alec cuddled beside me.

For the first and last time in my life I hated Alec, positively, for his brilliant white coat should have attracted any eye, let alone a sentinel's.

A moment went by, and then the fellow withdrew from the lookout position at the edge of the bank. Why he did not see us, I cannot tell. I cannot even dream. It was about the worst five seconds of my life, and I can only explain his blindness by the fact that he did not expect to find us there. He paid no more attention to us than a man would to a real emerald in a string of green glass. He marched back to the tent, hesitated, and then, after a glance all about him, he went inside.

I waited for two or three seconds only. Then I cautioned Alec to lie still, and I got up and began to creep forward.

The wind was icing my face, but that was not the coldest part of me. My heart was the thing that turned to stone. The guard might, as I hoped, have gone into the tent to lie down, feeling that further watching was not much good. Or, on the other hand, he might have gone in to waken another man who was to stand the last watch. Or he might be rousing the others to commence the day's work. Only in the first case would I be fairly safe. In either of the other instances, I would be advancing into a trap.

Well, I was straight in front of that tent and leaning over the pile of the dog harness, when a hand thrust back the flap of the tent. I saw the big, fuzzy mitten that covered the hand, and the sight struck my brain numb. I actually expected the guard to leap out at me.

Instead, the hand disappeared and the flap was allowed to fall again.

Then I understood. He had gone inside to fetch something and, having got it, he now remembered something else. That touch of remembering might be the salvation of Joe May!

I scooped up that harness in one sweep. It was hard with ice, stiff, and actually crackled like fire under my hands; but I slid back through the willows with that trailing armful, with a wild hope in my heart, and a shudder of cold dread in the small of my back, as though eyes were already fixed on me.

I slipped over the edge of the bank a half second

before the watcher came out the second time from the tent.

Crouching in my shelter, breathing with a deal of difficulty and biting my lips, I saw him stretch his big arms once or twice. Then I went on down the bank.

It would only be a moment before he noticed the disappearance of the harness, and probably two seconds later before he found my trail.

So I slid down that bank like an otter heading into a pool, and then I streaked up in the shadow of the bluff. Every step that I made was making a bigger margin of safety for me. Guns miss ten times as often at fifty yards as they do at twenty.

I got my fifty yards behind me before I dared to turn and look back.

Still, nothing showed over the edge of the bluff.

On I went. I ran with not quite all my might, because I had two miles before me—and that dreadful weight of trailing, tangling harness in my arms.

Still there was no sound from behind me!

At last, I turned and climbed to the top of the bank again. There I threw down my prize and I began to work with my knife. I sliced and slashed those harnesses to smithereens. I cut them vertically and then across the grain of the straps. Then I threw them away among the bushes. Only one harness I saved, for a use which I'll tell you about at once.

When I had finished this destruction, I went back to the edge of the bluff, expecting to find three dark forms streaking across the bright face of the ice, but again I was wrong.

I could not understand. If that watcher had sat down where he had been sitting before, of course he would instantly notice what was lacking. But perhaps he began to walk aimlessly up and down.

At any rate, my job was done, and done well, I thought. I got down that bank again to the ice, and there I slipped that harness onto Alec and took hold of the long pull strap myself.

He knew perfectly what I meant. Running home like that, with Alec pulling at a gallop, was a good deal like being blown along by a strong wind. And all the way, turning to look over my shoulder from time to time, I was more and more amazed, more and more delighted to see that no one had come out behind us.

Alec took me home, as I've been saying, helped me to climb the bank, and then went into the tent and stuck his cold nose into the neck of Massey.

We had that camp up and stirring in half a minute.

Working furiously, we struck camp. We bundled things loosely onto the sleds. We strung out the dogs, and hustled them out onto the ice.

Great Scott, how my heart jumped and my head grew dizzy when I saw three gigantic silhouettes coming up the river toward us, and not more than a quarter of a mile away.

Chapter Fifteen
Marjorie's Story

They had come up close in under the bluff, so that we did not see them till the last minute. Then, with yells, we started the dogs. The sleds were very lightly loaded by this time. The dogs could pull them and yank us along, too, at a good clip. But for a few minutes I thought that my legs would give way and that I'd have to fall flat on my face on the ice. Marjorie's head was back and wobbling from side to side as she raced along, and every breath that she drew was a groan. But finally the pace told on the three men running after us. The first I knew of it was the singing of a bullet past my ear, and then the sharp, thin echo flung after it across the ice.

Other bullets followed. One of the three carried a rifle, and he was kneeling on the ice behind us, taking careful shots.

However, mittens are bad things to shoot in and, be-sides, every one gets out of practice with guns during the long winter, when there's little or nothing to shoot at. These bullets went wild. A month later, at the same distance and the same targets, I suppose that very man would have dropped us, all three; but he missed, and we went around a bend to safety.

We could afford to settle down to a walk, then, and all that day we continued to slog along slowly. We had an enormous start on Calmont, now. Having failed in his spurt to catch us, he would have to go back to the camp, give up a large part of the load that remained, devise some sort of a harness for a few of the dogs, and then strike out after us once more. It was probable that he had some extra leather along but, if he had enough to hitch up more than three or four dogs, he was lucky.

Take it all in all, we had good reason to feel that the danger was over and that we were safe from Calmont from this time forward. We did not talk much about it, but words were not needed to express our relief and our happiness. To make everything perfect, the day was bright and clear and almost hot. We were tired, of course, and traveled very slowly, but that made no difference to us, because we were confident that Calmont was out of the picture. Another trouble, and about the only one we had, was the fact that the ice had been cut pretty thin in places by the action of the water from underneath. Sometimes we could feel the whole surface give under our weight, and a very sickening sensation it was. Sometimes, too, we could see open bits of water under cracks, and everything pointed to the breaking up of the Yukon at once. Well, we hardly cared, for in any case Calmont was lost behind us.

We found a good camping place in the evening and had a hearty meal. Even Massey seemed more cheerful than usual, and actually smiled once or twice. And Alec the Great, always in perfect sympathy with the humans around him, acted like a foolish, great puppy, rolling, pawing, nipping, begging, playing possum, walking on hind legs and front legs, and going through the hundred clowning tricks which Massey had taught him.

After dinner, I helped Marjorie wash and rebandage Massey's eyes. A frightful sight they were, the balls as red as fire, and all the skin around the eyes badly swollen and inflamed. The burning powder had been enough to scald the outer tough epidermis. Think what it must have done to the exquisite tenderness of the eyeball!

Massey was a hero. He never referred to his blindness in any way, never cursed his luck, never complained about the future; but I knew with absolute surety that as soon as he was away from us he would take his own life. He could endure the constant torment of those injured eyes—every flicker of an eyelid, no doubt, was an agony—and without a groan he could get through day after day; but now and again I was able to spot a stiffening of his lips and a hardening of his jaw muscles, and at those times I knew very well what was coming. He would stick out the journey with us, simply because he felt that it was his sporting duty to do so; but life held nothing ahead for him.

When we had bathed his eyes and made a poultice of tea leaves to put over them, Marjorie began to talk. She talked about me, at first. She said a good deal about what I had done that morning in spoiling Calmont's outfit. She talked about my courage, and such stuff; and Massey amazed me and made me feel like a king by announcing that it was a nervy job, and that I'd make a man, one day.

Once Marjorie's tongue was loosened, she went on. She said that she had intended keeping the secret to herself forever, but that we had come to mean so much to her that she had to put herself in a little better light than that of a thief and a sneak.

She sat up by the stove with her hands gripped hard together and her eyes flicking back and forth from me to Massey as she talked. It wasn't easy for her, but I knew that we were hearing truth. What she had to say was a pretty common story, all except her part of it. She had a sister by name of Joan who married the town's bright boy, a fellow called Lindley.

Lindley worked in the bank, got quick advancement, and was so valuable that it was said that he personally was responsible for getting half of the accounts which the bank carried. He built himself a good house and had the best of everything, and they appeared to be the happiest young couple in the state. They had two children. Everything was going along fine, to all appearances, when one evening Joan came to Marjorie, hysterical, and told her that there was a crash for fair.

Lindley had cleared out.

Well, of course, he had been spending too much, ran behind, gambled in stocks to make up losses, lost still more, swiped money from the bank for a final plunge, and woke up owing the bank over eight thousand dollars. Then he cleared out, leaving a letter in which he said that he would never come home until he could pay what he owed and clear his name.

They had no trace of him for a long time, and then a letter came to Marjorie from Alaska, from Lindley. It begged for news about Joan and the babies, and asked her not to mention the fact that he had gone to Nome.

She did what he asked. She said nothing, but she got her things together and went to Nome to try to persuade that brother-in-law of hers to go back to the States. He could change his name, if necessary, and start life over again, and save up money until he could pay off his debts, but to leave his wife and youngsters was bad business for them all.

Up to Nome she went, sure of her powers to persuade, but when she found Lindley, he was adamant and would not be budged. He was going to tear gold out of the frozen tundra if he had to do it with his teeth, he said.

It was after that interview that I found her crying at Tucker's house. She had made up her mind to do something desperate. If Lindley stayed there in Alaska, she was sure that he never would get what he needed; and in the meantime Joan's heart was breaking. It was a wild scheme that came to the girl's mind. But she had the stuff in her that martyrs are made of.

She saw Lindley again and told him that she had worked out a gambling system, that it paid big, and that she was going to make a killing with it. If he would meet her that night at a certain place, she would hand him the coin that he needed.

Poor Lindley! I suppose he was too desperate to ask questions or doubt. A miracle was promised to him, and he simply held out his hand and took the pot of gold that fell into it, while Marjorie walked on to throw her life away and, instead, stepped into my hands and into as odd a series of incidents as I've ever heard of.

Now, she told this yarn with a quick, quiet voice, and wound up with an apology for Lindley, saying that he was really a good sort, and all that kind of thing; but, while I listened to her, I thought that I was hearing from about as big a spirit as a boy or man could find in this world. There was a solemn sort of accompaniment for this talk, for outside, on the river, we could hear murmurings and boomings, and distant thunders, so that we knew the time had almost come when the Yukon would break up.

It might make hard work for us over the rough going

inland if we had to give up the ice road, but it would be a picture to see and remember. For Marjorie and me to see, I should say. There would be no picture on the darkened eyes of Massey, again.

When the story came to an end, Massey dropped his face in his hands. That amazed me, but a moment later light was shown to my blind eyes. For Marjorie waved me toward the tent flap.

Her face was white; her eyes were big; her lips were trembling. And I got out of that tent as fast as a hunted wolf out of a lamb fold.

On the outside, walking up and down with Alec, I turned the thing over in my mind. She was going to get out of Massey the confession that he cared for her and, once he spoke, I could guess that she was going to say that she loved him with her whole soul. I knew it suddenly and fully, as well as if I had heard her speaking the words.

Why this thing should be, I could not tell. He had been nothing but rude, brutally rude. The girl had been nothing to him, at least in the beginning, other than a bait to catch Calmont.

But I could guess that she had been able to look under the surface and see a finer picture of him than I had known. Even I had grown very fond of him; but Marjorie was wise enough and big enough to see into the heart of him.

It was like her to fall in love with a lost cause, of course. I could see that it was exactly the sort of thing to expect of her, and pity for her, and sorrow for Massey, choked me. I tried to look into their future, but all I could see was the darkness that lay in Massey's wounded eyes.

Perhaps the eyes would recover? Well, that would be almost too good to be true.

While I walked up and down, I heard nothing except once when Massey cried out in a terrible, great voice: "No, no, no!"

It sent shudders through me, for I could guess that he was trying to keep her from throwing herself away on a ruined life. Poor Massey!

When I was called back in by the girl, I found that Massey had slipped into his sleeping bag. And when I stared at Marjorie to read what I could, I saw that she was somewhere between tears and happiness. She must have persuaded a confession out of him; but I could imagine that she had not been able to break down his manhood enough to induce him to accept her self-sacrifice. He was not the sort to ruin the life of the woman he loved by becoming a burden to her.

This sight of the two of them, Massey with his face turned to the wall, was about as sad a thing as I've ever known.

Chapter Sixteen
Alec Gone!

I had a good sleep but not a very long one. Presently new, deeper, and nearer thunders roared out from the river, and I hurried out to the edge of the bluff. Marjorie was already there, and together we watched the thing.

The thawing had weakened the ice long enough so that the swelling force of the river was ripping it to pieces. Great slices, squares, and humps of ice went down the stream and, since we were on the point of a fairly sharp curve, sometimes a spin of the water shot a raft of ice against the bank with enough force to make the soil tremble beneath our feet.

Just in the middle of the bend, where the current was swiftest, stood a little island, and down on this came the ice sections in such number, size, and force that it looked as though the island would be crushed away to nothing.

The glistening floes, when they hit the rocks under water, leaped up as though they had life of their own, and with such a splintering, crashing, shattering and roaring that it sounded like the fall of cities.

It was not the ice alone that was impressive, however. The Yukon is a whopping big river, and now its muddy yellow water was boiling and frothing. It ran like children turned loose. Or, rather like herds of buffalo stampeding.

The winter is the great force, the long-enduring force, in that land, but here was the spring having its moment and shouting with delight over it. Such a singing and dancing was a tremendous thing to watch. It made one grin, and stare until the eyes popped out. Marjorie and I looked at one another from time to time, and smiled, and felt that life somehow was a pretty good thing.

I had just stretched out my arm to point at the approach of an extra big cake, when I was grabbed from behind, jerked about, and shown the business end of a Colt revolver. It looked as big as a cannon, and on the other end of that gun was Calmont!

I would not have been surprised if he had taken me by the legs and flung me into the river, but I was nothing in his mind. He passed me to one of the other men; a third was already taking charge of Marjorie, and holding a handkerchief over her mouth to keep her from making any sound.

Calmont, when his hands were free, stepped over to her.

"Now," says he, "you'll have a chance to see the wind-up of this dance you've started!"

And he marched off toward the tent.

I understood. He was going to fight it out with Massey. That was his plan. He could not know that there was a blind man inside that tent.

About ten yards from the entrance he stopped and shouted: "Massey!"

I made a sudden struggle, and the fellow who had

hold of me clipped me alongside the head with the barrel of his gun and promised to brain me if I tried to make a sound or give any warning. I looked across and saw Marjorie helplessly struggling, too. And the men who held us were grinning with expectancy. They apparently had perfect faith in Calmont's ability to win any fight.

Through my horror at what was to happen there was another emotion shot like a grand red color, and that was the magnificence of Calmont as he stood yonder in front of the tent with his revolver in his hand, waiting for his enemy to come out, confident that he would not be shot from ambush, but met face to face like a man. The concentrated essence of a perfect hate was the light in the face of Calmont, of course, but there was also something more.

Or perhaps even hatred may be sublime after it once passes a certain point.

What would that blind man do when he heard the voice of his enemy? Well, I knew that something terrible was about to happen, but I was not prepared for the actuality. In another instant, out rushed Massey with a revolver in his hand—and without the bandage across his eyes!

I thought, for a staggering instant, that he really had recovered his sight, but then I realized the truth. He wanted death, and the cheapest way to get it was at the hands of Calmont.

The man who was holding me had gripped me across the mouth to keep me still; but as Massey appeared, lunging out into the open and turning toward the voice of Calmont, I bit the hand that stifled me. The hand jumped away, and I yelled at the top of my lungs: "He's blind! Calmont, he's blind!"

I fairly shrieked it, but I thought that I was too late, for I saw the gun flashing up in Calmont's hand. Massey had raised his own weapon. There was a heavy explosion, but it was from Massey's revolver. He had fired, you see, toward the sound of Calmont's voice.

Perhaps that bullet flew very wide. Perhaps Calmont had heard my voice and believed me. At any rate, he held his fire, and then by slow degrees the weapon in his hand dropped back to his side. One thing was clear: that Calmont either wanted fair play, or that he loathed Massey so completely that the crushing of a blind man meant nothing to him.

Alec, springing out of the tent, behind his master, saw Calmont and winced to the side with a frightful snarl of hate and suspicion; but Massey, turning slowly about, fumbled his way back inside. I had a good glimpse of his face, and it certainly was blank with despair.

Calmont came over to the girl, and she and I were turned loose.

"You've got what you want," he said. "You've got your man . . . a fine kind of a man that'll make money out of a woman. But you got him, and may he do you a lot of good! You'll likely get sick of your blind beggar. But if you stick with him, you can pray that he never gets sight back into his eyes, for if he does, I'm gunna come and throttle him, with you standin' by to watch it! You. . . ."

He could not find the words he wanted. He turned around in a strangling fury and saw me. I thought that he would make a lunge at me, but his second glance measured me better and showed that I was not meat for him. He looked wildly about, and then uttered a deep-throated cry as he saw Alec.

There was his one reward. His long journey went for nothing. A blind man he could not attack, and as for the blind man's woman—for of course that's what he took Marjorie to be—he disdained her, or tried to. But he

116

caught up Alec and dragged the poor dog after him into the brush. He had to muzzle that husky in order to lead him along safely, for Alec was frantic. His yells and clamorings came back to us out of the brush after they were out of sight, and I felt as sick and miserable as though I were hearing a child crying out for help.

But I could do nothing against the three of them. They had come and gone all in a moment. They had not touched a thing of ours. I'm sure that the two brutes who marched with Calmont would have been glad to help themselves to our outfit, but they did not dare to act without orders. He had them perfectly in hand, and the whole trio disappeared, and the crying of poor Alec died off in the distance.

They had, in fact, found enough material to patch up four dog harnesses, and a long, forced march told the rest of the story.

We listened to them going, Marjorie and I, as we stood there on the bank of the Yukon, staring at the great shoals of ice which had piled up on the island. But we were not thinking of the river. We were thinking of the blinded man in the tent. He was broken, even as the river was breaking.

Then a great wall of ice sailed around the curve, one of those barriers that form in the fall. This mass crashed against the ice jam with a roar like a thousand great guns. The whole obstruction was swept away, and the very bank under us quivered like a jelly.

As the uproar died out a little, and I watched the fragments shooting past, Marjorie said to me: "You go in to him first, Joe. Then I'll come a little later."

I knew what she meant. She was prepared to face a life of torment, of quiet martyrdom; but she loved the man well enough to undertake it. Only she wanted one quiet moment to prepare and nerve herself.

So I, with head down, went miserably and slowly toward the tent. Like the girl, I knew what was inside it, and I dreaded and loathed worse than death to look into the face of that broken man.

Chapter Seventeen
What the Doctor Thinks

Threading a needle with gloves on is a hard job. But I would rather try to thread a needle than handle a rifle with the sort of mittens that one wears in the arctic. In the first place, it is hard to crowd the forefinger inside of the trigger guard, and I worked and worked at my own pair until I managed to construct a finger cover that was smaller without being thin enough to allow a finger to grow cold. Furthermore, I got Jerry Payson, who used to be a blacksmith, to make a much larger guard. It looked like nothing much, that guard, when it was finished, but it was roomy and comfortable, and exactly what I wanted for the occasion. I had Jerry make two pairs, because I wanted one for my own rifle and an extra one for Massey's, in case he should regain his eyesight.

After Jerry finished the guards and put them on the rifles, I took mine outside of Circle City to do some practicing. I had just finished a hard freighting trip to

Forty Mile, and now I had some time out while we waited to get a new job. Even with the bigger guard, I found the rifle wonderfully clumsy. It seemed to slip and give, and it would not fit snugly against the shoulder, because of the thickness of the coat that I had on. Well, no matter for inconveniences, a fellow will put up with them when he feels that his life is going to depend upon the makeshift, one day.

I had drilled away six times at a willow at fifty yards before I hit the trunk fairly, and the shock of the bullet whizzing through dislodged a chunk of snow frozen into an upper fork of the little tree. When that lump fell, what do you think? A snowshoe rabbit jumped up and skidded for safer country. That rabbit had been lying low there all the time I put the whiz of five bullets over his head! But as Massey used to say, a rabbit is such a fool that it is almost a genius.

I swung the gun around and tried for that rabbit, but he did a spry hop just as I pulled the trigger. I tried again, and though he swerved as I fired, the bullet was going faster than his tricky legs, and he rolled over heels—a good fresh meal for Massey and me, I hoped.

I was about to start for that jack, when a voice said behind me: "Wasting ammunition this far north, Joe May?"

I turned around short and saw Doctor Hector Forman right behind me. He must have sneaked up while I was shooting but, for that matter, he was so small and light that it was no wonder he could get across the snow without making much noise.

I looked at him with an odd feeling, as I always had since he began to take care of Massey. Partly, I respected and liked him for the time he was spending on Massey— probably for nothing. Partly, I was afraid and suspicious of him. For he looked like a red fox, all sharp nose and bright eyes. He never could keep from smiling as he talked, as though he knew all about what went on inside one's mind and found it ridiculous. He was the most unpleasant fellow I ever knew, in lots of ways, but he was a bang-up doctor. Charitable, too, and the good he had done in Circle City you hardly would believe.

For that matter, most doctors are apt to be a little hard boiled. They have to see men and women in their worst moments, and they're likely to grow cynical.

"I was just having a little fun," I said.

He nodded at me. He was always nodding, no matter what any one said, as though he understood what you said and what you had in the back of your mind.

"Pretty far north for that kind of fun," he said.

I kicked at the snow and said nothing. What was there to say?

"Ammunition makes heavy luggage," he said, "and at a dollar a pound for freight, I don't see how you can afford to bring in so much of it."

"Aw, I don't bring in much," I said.

"I've seen you out here a dozen times if I've seen you once," he said, "and every time you've shot off enough powder and lead to keep a whole tribe in caribou meat for the winter."

"Well, I gotta have my fun," I said.

He nodded at me again. "A man ought to live near water," he said, "if he expects his house to catch on fire."

He waited for me to say something. I could only scowl and wish that I'd never met him. He went on, asking questions, mostly. That was his way. He made every one who talked to him feel like a patient.

"You've just come in from a trip?" he said.

"Yes," I said.

"Good pay?"

"Pretty good."

"And all the profits to be spent on Massey again, I suppose?"

I shrugged my shoulders and was silent.

"What did Massey ever do for you?" said the doctor.

"Aw, he just took me in when I was starving. That's all," I said. For it made me mad, this hard, critical, probing way of Forman's.

"How old are you?" he said.

"Twenty," I said, and looked him in the eye.

But it was no good. He knew that I was lying, and he merely grinned at me.

"Twenty," he said, and nodded once more. "But pretty soon you'll hear from the girl, and she'll send up enough money to get Massey out of Alaska."

"What girl?" I said.

"Why Massey's girl," he said.

I scowled at him, blacker than ever. "I don't know nothing about that," I answered.

"No, you wouldn't," said Forman, dry as a chip. He shrugged his shoulders to settle the furs closer to his skinny, shivering body.

"You come out here to see me about something?" I asked.

"Me? No, I just wanted to see the shooting," he said.

He smiled, to let me see openly that he did not mean what he said. But I knew that already.

"This all started about a dog, I believe?" he said.

"A dog?" I asked him, dodging as well as I could.

"You don't know anything about that either, do you?" he said.

I stared at him.

"Isn't it a fact," he said, "that Calmont and Massey were once great friends?"

I said nothing. Of course, all Alaska knew that.

"And that they spent a winter out from Nome, and that one of Calmont's dogs in the team had a litter, and that Alec the Great was one of the puppies."

"I don't know nothing about that," I said.

"The rest of the country does, though," he said.

"That's none of my business," I said.

"Murder is every man's business, my boy," he barked at me suddenly.

I winced. It was an ugly word, but it fitted the case.

"That dog grew attached to Massey, not to Calmont," went on the doctor, hard and sharp as ever. "They fought about Alec, finally, and Calmont laid him out, and tied him on the floor of the igloo, and went off to leave him to starve or die of cold. Is that wrong? No, it's not wrong! And then the dog broke away from Calmont and got back to Massey, and somehow, Massey managed to get free of the cords, though I don't believe what people say when they tell that Alec chewed the cords away to set the man free. Do you?"

I stared at him again. "Well," I said, "you don't know Alec as well as I do."

"All right," went on the doctor. "The fact is that Massey got back to Nome with the dog, which Calmont claimed, but the jury in Nome awarded the dog to the man it loved, eh? Touching idea, that!"

He gave a cackling laugh and clapped his hands together.

"Now, what's the rest of the story, my lad?" he said.

"Well, I don't know," I said.

"I'll tell you, then," he said. "A girl shows up in Nome in a desperate need of money, and sells herself to the highest bidder. To be the wife of the man able to bid her in, eh? Now, then, Calmont is the man who gets her, for eleven thousand dollars. A high-priced wife, even this far north! Can't eat wives . . . or diamonds either, for that matter. And after the girl's sold, you and Massey steal her away and cart her south, and Massey's hope is that Calmont will overtake them and the two of them can fight it out. But, on the way, he takes a few practice shots, and with one of them he burns his eyes with a back fire. Is that right?''

"Massey can tell you better than I can," I said.

"Then Calmont does overtake you. He finds Massey blinded. He won't take the girl in spite of the way she's double-crossed him. He won't take a woman who loves another man, eh?''

I only shrugged again. It was pretty clear that he knew nearly everything. I suppose that he had ways of finding out part of it, and the rest he guessed. He had a brain in his head, no matter what I felt about him.

"But he does take that dog, Alec the Great, and you and Massey and the girl come on here. She goes south the first chance she gets, to rake together money and send it to you two for the trip out. You stay here to take care of Massey. And Massey sits still and eats his heart out because of Alec the Great. Am I still correct?''

"I got nothing to say," I said.

"Now, then," went on Forman, "if I succeed in my work, and if Massey sees again, the first thing that he will do will be to take the trail of Calmont. There'll be a fight. And most likely the pair of them will be killed. They're too tough to die easily. Very well, that's the reason that you're out here practicing with your rifle. You have an idea that you'll be traveling on the trail with Massey, before long.''

I sighed at this. It was perfectly true.

"Well," I said, "is he going to be able to see?''

Forman puckered up his face, and swayed his head from side to side.

"If I let him see, I'll practically be responsible for the

lives of two men . . . to say nothing of a boy or two thrown in for full measure. I imagine that there wouldn't be much left of you, if you were tangled up in a battle between that couple, eh?''

I shuddered. It was exactly my own idea.

''Well,'' said Forman, ''I don't think there's much wrong with his eyes, after all. It was a shallow burn. At any rate, I'm taking the bandages off in about five minutes, if you care to come along and see the result.''

Care to come along? I ran at Forman and caught him by the arm.

''D'you mean that Hugh Massey has a good chance?'' I shouted at him.

He grinned sourly down at me. ''Considering what's likely to follow, do you think that you'd be glad of it?'' he said.

That stopped me. He was right. I hardly knew whether to be glad or sorry.

Chapter Eighteen
How Repay?

We went back into that silent town, the doctor slipping clumsily on his snowshoes. I wonder whatever could have brought him up here into the bitter, long winter of Alaska, he was so unfit for the life.

He had only one quality of the frontiersman, a bitter, hard temper that never gave way. But as for strength, vitality of body, youth—he had none of these things at all. Nevertheless, he was an exceptional man, as he had just proved by recounting to me almost the entire strange story of Calmont and Massey. Of course, some of the headlines, as one might say, of that story, had been known to every one for a long time—that is, such features as that they had once been great friends and that they had afterward become great enemies and that only the blinding of Massey had prevented the final battle between them.

There were some people who swore that the only reason Massey remained in Alaska was not that he couldn't get out, but because he wanted to be close to Calmont and his chance for revenge. Well, I suppose I knew Massey about as well as any one in the world did—outside of Calmont himself—but Massey was not a talking man, and he never had made a confidant of me. I don't think that he ever would have paid much attention to me, if it had not been for the fact that I once helped Alec the Great from a mob of hungry huskies.

So, as we went along, I kept giving this doctor side glances, for I half felt that he was more fiend than human.

As we passed Don Lurcher's house, we heard them shouting and singing inside. They had their own supply of alcohol in that place, and the amount of noise that they squeezed out of themselves through the entire winter was a thing to hear, but not to believe. Everything else was cold, white, and still, for the soft snow ate up the sound of the footfall, except for the little metallic squeaks and crunchings, now and again.

We got to our shack.

It was a fairly comfortable one, with very thick walls of logs that had been rafted down the Yukon. On the outside of the logs, there was a thick layer of sod, which helped to turn the edge of the wind.

Inside, everything was fixed up pretty well. There were two comfortable bunks, and a stove that was not big, but that heated that little place as well as the sun ever heated the earth on a spring morning, say. Yes, we were pretty comfortable—for Circle City.

But there was one figure in the shack that was not at all comfortable to see. I had looked at him every day for months—except when I was making a freighting trip—and I never could get used to the sight.

I mean Massey.

The grim, enduring look that pinched the corners of

his mouth never had altered since the first day of his blindness. Of course, he could not read, so I often read aloud to him. And he had only one occupation all the day long. That was to keep himself fit, and how he did it!

Once he had been more tiger than man. He was not very big, but I never saw more concentrated essence of sheer power than he showed. Calmont, perhaps, was stronger in his hands, but then Calmont was a good deal bigger. When the pair of them were together as friends in the old days, there was a saying in Skagway—when Skagway was toughest—that the two of them were equal to any four in the world in a rough and tumble. And I believe the legend.

Now, Massey spent long hours every day doing calisthenics, and we had rigged a bar across one corner of the room on which he performed all the antics of a monkey on the branch of a tree.

That was to keep himself right and in trim, and why? Well, he never spoke about it, but I knew. Massey felt that he had one chance in ten of getting back his eyesight. And if ever that returned, he did not want to find himself soft. He wanted to start immediately on the trail of Calmont.

He was fit as a fiddle, therefore, physically, and I've always thought that this good training kept him from going despondent as he sat there through his long night.

This day the doctor said as we went in: "Well, Massey, how are things going?"

Massey lifted his head and nodded. "I can't complain," he said.

"Complaints never cured a wound, though tears may have washed a few," said the doctor in his harsh voice. "I'm moving to take the bandage off you, now. Boy, close that door, and put a blanket over the window. Too much light might be a torment to him . . . if he's going to see!''

Massey said not a word. I went to do as I was told, trembling with excitement, and that confounded Forman was whistling idly as he laid out his things on the deal table in the center of the room. He had no more soul than a snake, I thought at the time.

With the door closed, and the window veiled, there was no more light in that room than the red streaks that showed around the stove, and one glowing spot where the handle of the damper fitted into the thin chimney.

Then I stood by, waiting, while the doctor worked at the bandages. He said: ''Keep your eyes closed while I take the bandage off. Then open your eyes very slowly.''

I saw a movement of the dull shadows, as the doctor did something with his hands and then stepped back. And suddenly Massey stood up.

Neither of them spoke for a long moment. My heart got so big that I thought it would break.

''Huh!'' I screamed out suddenly. ''Can you see? Can you see anything?''

Now, imagine that man having sat there through the dull, endless hours of every day, looking at the empty thought of his young, ruined life, with no more hope for the future than a drowning man where help is not in sight—imagine that, and then conceive of the iron grip that he kept on himself.

He answered in the calmest voice in the world: ''I can see perfectly, Forman. Thank you.''

''Take the blanket off the window, boy,'' said Forman.

I did it.

And now I could see the unveiled eyes of Hugh Massey for the first time, with recognition in them as he looked at me. Even this dim twilight through the window, however, was almost too much for him, and he shaded his eyes as he looked at me.

I have never seen anything so exciting. The Yukon breaking up in the summer was nothing compared to the making of this man whole again. I ran to him and shook his hand. I threw my arms around him and hugged him. I laughed. I shouted. Tears of pure joy ran down my face, and in general I played the fool.

But Massey was as calm as steel.

When he talked, it was to the doctor. He said that he realized he owed a great deal to the doctor, and that it would not be forgotten.

"Massey," said the doctor, with such a changed voice that I should not have recognized the sound of it, "up there in Nome, one evening, old 'Doctor' Borg, as they called him, made you and Calmont swear that you never would attack one another. What about it now?"

"Attack him, Forman?" said Massey, very gently. "Why, I never would think of breaking my word ... unless he attacks me. Of course, a man is allowed to defend himself. Am I right?"

"Do you think Calmont will come hunting you?"

"Do I think? Oh, I know! Besides, I'll probably not be hard to find."

"You mean what?"

"Why, man, I simply mean that Calmont has a dog of mine! Keeping it for me, as you might say. Of course, I'll have to go to get the dog back. Calmont's over on Birch Creek, I believe?"

The doctor said nothing. He got on his coat and went to the door, which he jerked open. As he stood there in the entrance, he half turned, and he snapped over his shoulder:

"If there's murder in this business, I, for one, wash my hands. They're clean of it!"

A staggering thing, in a way, to hear from him. I mean to say, all at once I realized that under his hard exterior the doctor was a law-abiding man, and that he actually was interested in something higher and stronger than human law, at that.

Massey, when the door closed, went over to the stove and took off the lid. Shading his eyes and squinting, he looked down into the red heart of the fire. Then, as though this satisfied him in a way that I could not understand, he replaced the lid and returned to his bunk, where he sat down.

I said nothing, this while. I was somewhere between joy in the moment and fear for what was to come.

At last he said to me: "Well, old son, we're together again, at last!"

As though we had been apart all these weeks and months! But I knew what he meant. Whole mountain ranges of misery had grown up between him and the rest of the world, even including me.

"I can't really wish," he said, "for you to get into the state that I've been in but, otherwise, I don't think that I can ever repay you, Joe."

It was the first time that he ever had said so much as "thank you." I had almost thought, at times, that he was taking everything for granted. But that hardly mattered, because I had owed my life to him, that horrible day, long ago, in Nome.

But this gratitude, from a man of iron, affected me a good deal more than I can explain. I merely said: "It's all right, Hugh. There doesn't have to be any talk about repaying . . . not between you and me."

He considered this for a moment in his deliberate way. Then he answered: "No, I never could repay. I've been helpless in your hands. You've had to nurse me, feed me by hand, shave me, dress me, partly. There never can be any repaying. Except with bloodshed!'' he added in an off inflection. ''Except with bloodshed, Joe, old fellow!''

The tears were in my eyes, listening to him. I knew exactly what he meant. And I knew that he was a man to be believed. And it's not a light thing to hear such a man as Massey say that he's ready to die for you—almost anxious to.

''We're only even,'' I said. ''I don't forget that day in Tucker's boarding house in Nome. I'll never forget that!''

At this, he laughed a little. ''All right,'' he said. ''We'll talk no more about it.''

And from that day, we never did.

Chapter Nineteen

Welcome to Dawson

Of course, Circle City knew all about the affairs of Massey and Calmont or enough, at least, to expect the sparks to fly so soon as ever the pair of them met, and the expectation got high and drawn. But, in the meantime, Massey was as calm and deliberate as you please.

There were several things that he wanted to do. He used to talk matters over with me, and I would sit listening, with my eyes popping.

In the first place, he wanted to get his eyes accustomed to light, and his hands accustomed to a gun.

In the second place, he wished to wait until the Yukon was frozen, which would make distance traveling a lot easier. Already the ice was forming and floating in blocks and jams down the river, like white logs. Hardly an hour went by without giving us the vibration and the thunder of a shoal of ice, grounding against an island. The cold got greater and greater, and Massey went into

133

the pinch of it regularly, giving himself larger and larger doses, so that he would become inured.

In the third place, he said to me: "Even a rattlesnake gives you a warning, and so I'll give one to poor Arnie."

He had a fiendish way of giving pet names and speaking gently about Calmont. He used to smile with a very peculiar sweetness when he talked about Calmont, and I hated to face him or to hear him, at such times. This warning he sent in due time.

He wrote out a letter and spent a lot of time composing it, and making the copy neat. He showed it to me with anxiety, hoping that I would point out anything that might be wrong about it.

This is the way it ran:

Dear Arnie:

> **It's a long time since I've seen you, and I haven't had a chance to thank you for the good care that you've been giving to Alec all this time. He must have grown, but I hope that he'll remember me.**

> **However, now I can see again, and I may be of use to Alec, and he to me. If you are coming in to Circle City, let me know. Otherwise, I'll come out there to call on you and to get my dog.**

> **Please figure out your bill. I have an idea as to how much I owe you, but I would like to know exactly what you think on the same point.**

> **Always thinking of you,**

> **Hugh Massey.**

This letter gave me a chill. It sounded so friendly, I mean, and there was such a purring malice between the lines. Why, that letter would have fooled any outsider, I suppose, but of course it would not fool Calmont. He knew that the one comfort Massey could have had in his blindness would have been the dog. And he knew that all Massey owed him was a perfect and gigantic hatred. However, this note was sent off to Birch Creek by a man who was just starting out in that direction.

We waited for word to come back. Calmont probably would not overlook this warning. He would come in or else he would ask Massey to go out.

Gun practice went on every day outside of the town with Massey using a revolver or a rifle like a master. I was a clumsy hand with any gun, compared with him. He had a natural talent for weapons, and he had cultivated his gifts.

Even when he was back in the shack, he used to do knife tricks, throwing a heavy hunting knife across the width of the room into the trunk of a sapling not two inches thick. I almost began to think that the knife would be his best weapon at close quarters.

His spirits were rising, all this while. The prospect of the fight that was coming was like a secret joy constantly being whispered into his ears.

He told me that I was to leave him. I could have half of the dog team and wait there in Circle City, in case he had to go out and find Calmont. That was what I wanted to do; but I pointed out that Calmont had a new partner up on Birch Creek, and that the odds would be two to two, no matter how the fight came off. He admitted this, but he swore that he would never let me get into action on his behalf.

This problem haunted me.

To go on the trail of Calmont was a nightmare to me in prospect, but I did not see how I could let Massey go out there by himself to fight two men. Two pairs of eyes are a lot better than one, and so are two guns, even though young hands are gripping one of them. It was my duty, according to the code, to go with Massey when the pinch came.

The code I mean is the law of the frontier, where the fellow who leaves his bunkie in the lurch is branded for all his life. A year before this, I would still have been young enough to escape from too much blame. But now I was seventeen, and pretty well hardened and bronzed by that last year of Northern life, so that I looked older than the fact. I was treated like a man. I had been doing a man's work in the freighting, and I would be expected to act like a man in the extreme pinch.

Well, duty is as cold a judge as Judge Colt. It held me up, but it made me mighty queer in the pit of the stomach.

Finally, I said to him, one evening: "Look here, Hugh. Suppose you were standing in my boots. What would you do? Would you let yourself be left behind? What would people think of me? They know that Calmont has a partner."

"Oh, dang what people think!" said Massey.

But he said this without conviction and, after that, he talked very little on the subject.

I found a couple of men in Circle City who knew Calmont's partner, however, and from them I got a good description of the man who was to be my half of the fight. A tough bit of meat for any man's eating was what he sounded to me.

Sam Burr was his name. Down around the Big Bend country they still remember him. He had a reputation there so bad that there was a time when any decent man could have taken a shot at Sam Burr without being so much as arrested for a killing that everybody thought was needed. The truth is that Sam was not quite right in the head, to my way of thinking. He was a mental defective. The only thing that gave him any real pleasure was fighting. And his idea about fighting was that of an Indian of the true old school. A bullet through the back was better than a bullet through the forehead. To stalk a man like a beast gave him the joy of a beast. As a matter of fact, there was Indian blood in him, and, like some half-breeds, he had the bad qualities of both bloods.

I asked why Calmont had ever hitched himself up to a man of that caliber.

"I guess," said the fellow who was telling me, "that Calmont needed some excitement, when there was no Massey on his trail. He picked up Sam Burr, and Sam will sure be a hypodermic for him!"

They said that he was a thin, stringy man, a great runner and packer, and a natural-born gunfighter.

So, from that moment, I had nightmares, and day horrors, with a thin-faced, dark-eyed fellow always playing the part of the fiend to toast me on the coals of my imagination.

The Yukon was well frozen over, when surprising word came in from Birch Creek that Calmont was no longer there. It made a sensation in Circle City. Calmont had pulled out some time before, and rumor said that he had trekked for the Klondike, and that he and Sam Burr had staked out a claim not on Bonanza Creek, but on another run of water not far away.

I was the one who brought news of this rumor to Massey, and I saw his features contract and a perfectly fiendish hate and malice come into his eyes.

I knew his thought. He was wondering whether or not Calmont had heard of his cure, and had purposely cleared out of our neck of the woods; but a moment of reflection was enough to clear away that doubt. Calmont would not run a mere couple of hundred miles, or so. He would go two thousand, at least, if he wanted to get rid of Massey permanently.

Massey said nothing at the time. He only took a couple of turns through the shack, and went to bed early that evening. I did the same, after getting my pack together, because I guessed that we would be making an early start.

We were, as a matter of fact. We got out after about five hours' sleep, and I started catching up the dogs. Massey wanted to stop me.

He said: "Old son, what kind of a man would I be if I let you go along on this little job and get your head shot off?"

"What sort of a man would I be," I said, "if I let you go, with both Calmont and Sam Burr ahead of you?"

"Oh, Sam is no job at all, Joe," he said. "He won't trouble me at all."

"Then he'll be easy for me," I said. "If you stop me, Hugh, I'll follow along after you without dogs."

"Well," he said, "Dawson will be a better place to argue this."

Afterward, I found out what he meant by that. At the time, I really thought he spoke only words.

We hit the river ice. It was new and slick and smooth, but pretty dangerous in spots. But we had six dogs in our team, two having died, and those six were as fast and strong a lot as I ever saw. Then we had a leader who was a marvel, and could read the mind of the ice, not like Alec the Great, but about as well as any other dog I ever saw.

Day by day, as the trip progressed, the ice got stronger and safer. We marched ourselves into high spirits, too.

The weather was good; the dogs were well and strong;

we had good camps. Plenty of tea and flour and bacon, and under circumstances like those, conditions were about as good as a man could ask for. It doesn't take much to make a man happy, when he's been used to the arctic. It's the absence of misery rather than the presence of comforts that counts.

As we got along up the river, on excellent going and with the ice growing thicker every moment, Massey was so happy that I found him with a contented smile on his face, more than once. Besides, he was often humming. And it's rare that you catch an Alaska dog-puncher in such a frame of mind, or ready to waste any energy on music making. For my part, I just closed my eyes to tomorrow and took every moment as it came.

At last we got up to sight of Dawson itself, a glad thing to Massey, and a horrible one to me. That huddle of houses dwindled in my eyes and I half expected that a gigantic form would stride out from it, wearing the wolfish face of that fellow Calmont.

We passed the mouth of the Klondike. It was fully a hundred yards from bank to bank, and its currents rushed along so fast that there was only a thin sheathing of ice across the top, though the Yukon was well crusted over. But the Klondike was only beginning to freeze, the black ice covering it with a sort of white dust. There were distinct sled marks up this creek, and the tracks went out at a big, irregular break. There was no need to ask what had happened to some poor puncher, sled, dogs, and all.

That, you might say, was our welcome to Dawson.

Chapter Twenty
Sam Burr

At this time, Dawson was running pretty wild. It was not as bad as Nome, because Dawson lies in Canada, and the Mounted Police had their eye on the place. There are police and police, but the Northwest Mounted were always all by themselves. Three of them were worth thirty of any other kind, unless it were the Texas Rangers, in their palmy days. Still, Dawson was so full of pep, and people, and money, that it was hard even for the Mounted to keep the town in order.

Imagine what had happened.

Men who had starved and toiled on Birch Creek and thanked Heaven for twenty-five-cent pans were now up there on the Klondike washing five and six hundred dollars to a pan. They had their smudgy fires going to thaw out the soil down to bed pan, and there they literally scooped out the treasure. Money came in so fast that the men did not know what to do with it.

We got into Dawson when everything was in full

blast. The strange thing was that there was so little talk about claims and gold. Gold was everywhere. It was like dirt under the feet. But imagine dirt that is dynamite, and that men will sell their souls for.

People talked about "outside," and the news they had got out of papers two months old, and which was the prettiest girl in such and such a dance hall, and whose dog would pull the heaviest load, and which dog was the smartest leader, but there was not so much talk about gold. If you heard a man talking at the bar about the richness of such and such a claim, you could put it down that he was trying to sell that claim, and that it was probably a blank.

Not always.

Right after we got to Dawson, we went into the Imperial bar and got some food and bought a drink. Not that Massey was a drinking man, but because that was the only way to enter into talk, and it was gossip about big Calmont that he wanted to hear.

Just after we had lined up at the bar, a fellow came in whom the bartender knew.

Their talk went something like this:

"Hello, Jack," said the bartender.

"Hullo, Monte," said the miner.

His face was covered with six inches of hair. His furs were worn through at the elbows and patched with sackcloth. He was the toughest, most miserable-looking man that I ever saw.

"How's things?" said the bartender.

"Fair to middling," said Jack. "How's things?"

"Busy," said Monte. "Down for a rest?"

"Down to quit," said Jack.

"Got through the gold dirt?"

"Naw, it's panning faster'n ever. But I'm tired."

"Of what?"

"Gold," said Jack.

I gaped at him. But nobody else seemed to notice. Imagine a man being tired of gold! And such a man—looking like a second-hand clothes dealer.

"What you taken out?" said Monte.

"About fifty thousand dollars," said Jack. "Gimme another and have one with me."

"I ain't drinking. But here's yours. Is fifty thousand your pile?"

"Yeah, that's about right."

"Couldn't use no more?"

"No more than that. Twenty thousand for the ranch that I want down there in Colorado, and thirty thousand to blow thawing out the ice that's been froze into me up here in Bonanza Creek."

"Gunna sell the claim?"

"Yeah, I reckon."

"What's your price?"

"I dunno. Whatever I can get for it."

Well, I heard afterward that Jack sold his claim for fifteen thousand dollars, but he did not leave Dawson with his money. He was not robbed, either. But he got too much whisky aboard and gambled his whole sixty-five thousand dollars away in a week. The people that bought the claim for fifteen thousand dollars on straight hearsay cleaned up another fifty thousand in a few weeks out of it, while Jack went up the creek and located again. This time he stayed for three months, and came out with a hundred thousand flat. He was lucky, of course. But there were a good many stories like this floating around when I was in the Klondike. People got so that gold, as I said before, was not really interesting. You have to translate the metal into houses, acres, clothes, jewels, and such things, before it grows exciting, and it was hard to visualize home comforts when in Dawson.

This yarn of Jack's about his profits made my eyes pop, but my interest did not last, for I knew that there was something else that meant a lot more to me.

It was the news about big Calmont. Out of that same bartender we got it.

"Partner," said Massey in his gentle, persuasive voice, "know anybody around here by the name of Calmont?"

The bartender was spinning out a row of eight glasses down the bar, and the way he gave those glasses a flip and made them walk into place was a caution. Then he fished out two glasses and rocked them down the bar the same way. He was proud of his art and too busy to pay much attention to Massey.

"Partner," said Massey again, "I just asked you a question about Arnie Calmont. D'you know him?"

"Busy!" barked Monte.

Massey reached a hand across the bar and taps the other on the shoulder.

The fellow jumped as though a gun had been nudged against his tender flesh.

"Hey, what's the matter?" he said.

"I was asking for a little conversation," said Massey.

Monte gave him a look, and gave me a look, too. What he saw in me did not matter. There was a certain air about Massey that was enough for him.

"Calmont's up the creek," he said.

"Where?"

"Not on Bonanza. Off in the back country. I dunno where. Sam Burr could tell you that."

"Where's Sam Burr? With Calmont?"

"No, he's over to Parson's boarding house."

Massey did not stop to thank Monte or to finish the whisky. He turned on his heel and strode from the room, with me at his heels.

143

We found Parson's boarding house, a low, dingy dive, and asked for Burr. He was there, all right.

"Are you doctors?" asked the fellow who met us at the door.

We said that we were not, but that we wanted a friendly word with Burr.

"Calmont ain't sent you?"

"No, we sent ourselves."

With that, he took us into a small room where I had my first sight of Sam Burr. He was all that I had expected to find him. He was simply a lean, greasy, good-for-nothing half-breed, with poison in his eye. When I had a look at the yellow whites of his eyes, I was glad that I was not apt to have to stand up against him with a gun, a knife, or even empty hands. He looked tricky enough to lick Jim Jeffries, just then, and that was when Jeff was knocking them cold. However, he was not apt to be doing any fighting, for a time. He lay in his bunk with some dingy blankets wrapped around him. There was a bandage around his head and a settled look about him that told he had been badly hurt.

This fellow lay back in his bunk, as I've said, and looked us over at his leisure. He had been reading a dog-eared old magazine, which he lowered and stared at us curiously. He was like a savage dog that stands in its own front yard and wonders whether you'll come close enough to have your throat cut. That was the calm, grim way that he drifted his glance over us.

"Hullo," said Massey.

Sam Burr made a slight movement with his hand that could have been taken to mean anything—and it was clear that he didn't care how we interpreted it.

"You're not with Calmont," said Massey.

"Unless he's under the bunk," said Burr.

He was one of those cool, sneering fellows. I hated

144

him at the first glance, and hated him twice over the moment that he spoke.

Massey went closer to him.

"Do you know me, Burr?" he said.

"No," said Burr. "I ain't got that . . . pleasure."

Why, he had to sneer and scowl at everything. Whatever he touched had to be made sticky with his tarry innuendoes.

"My name is Massey," said Hugh.

This jolted Burr in the right place. He let out a grunt and blinked up at us.

"You're Massey? You're the fellow!" he said.

"You busted with Calmont?" asked Massey.

"I'm gunna finish him," declared Sam Burr. "I'm gunna get even with him. He jumped me!"

"Is he here in Dawson?"

"Ah," said Burr, staring at Massey thoughtfully, "you want him all right, but I dunno that you'll get him. He's a hard case, that fellow Calmont."

Massey dismissed the idea of difficulty. His nerves were as tight as strings on a drum. He showed it. Have you ever seen a hound trembling against the leash?

"Well, he ain't here," said Burr at last.

"Where is he, then?"

"Up the creek."

"Can you tell me where?"

"Yeah. I can tell you where. I reckon that I will, too."

"Good," said Massey, and sat down.

He seemed more at ease, now, and spared time to ask: "What was the trouble?"

"Why, you wouldn't believe!" answered Sam Burr. "There we was getting along pretty good. He's a grouch, but so am I. We done fine together. But he exploded all account of a dang dog that he has along with him, or that he used to have. Alec the Great, is what I mean.''

Massey rose up from the chair as though some hand were pulling him by the hair of the head.

"Used to have?" he said.

"Yeah," said Burr, not noticing the excitement. "He set a fool lot on that dog, and it was the meanest, sulkiest brute that I ever seen. Had to be muzzled. Would've took Calmont's heart out as quick as a wink. I took him out on the lead, one day, and the beast whirled and tried for my throat. Nacherally, I let the lead strap loose, and off he went. When Calmont heard of that, he near went crazy. He jumped me when I wasn't looking. . . .''

Then he saw Massey's face and paused.

Chapter Twenty-one
On the Trail

Well, he had the best sort of a reason for stopping. I had seen Massey excited and angry before, but never so white and still, with his eyes burning in his face. Of course, Burr would not understand, but I did. There were three purposes in Massey's mind.

One was to marry Marjorie, when he got out of the country to the south.

One was to kill Calmont.

And the third was to get back Alec the Great.

Of the three, there was no doubt as to which stood at the head of the list. It was Alec the Great.

That doesn't talk down about his hatred of Calmont, either, or his love for Marjorie. Both those things were real, but Alec was something unique. He loved that dog like a friend, like a child, and like a dog, all in one. They had been through trouble together, of course. Not so many men can say honestly that they owe their lives to the brains and the teeth of a dog, but Massey could say that. Besides, he had a natural talent for animals, and I've seen him hold a long conversation with Alec, and Alec understanding most of the words.

Much as he wanted the life of Calmont, he wanted Alec the Great still more. Now he stood there white and still, looking down at Sam Burr, until the half-breed gaped up at him.

"Where is Calmont now?" asked Massey through his teeth.

"Why, up on the claim, I guess . . . unless he's gone off through the woods trying to find that dang murdering dog!"

"Where's the claim?"

"Up on Pension Creek."

"Where on the creek?"

"It's the only one on Pension Creek, and you can't miss it."

"Thanks," said Massey, and started for the door.

"Mind you," sang out Sam Burr, "I been saving that gent for myself! But if you're gunna try to help yourself first to him, leave a little for me. And be careful. He's kept in good gun practice!"

Massey gave no reply to this, but went off through the doorway, with me fairly treading on his heels. He led the way back to the sleds, and there he said: "We'll not go on together, son. We'll make an even split right here, and you wait for me here with your half. Wait for ten days and, if I'm not back by that time, I'll never be back, I reckon."

I argued that I would have to stay with him, but he was like a stone, at first, and went on dividing up everything, until we had two equal loads and two dog teams, instead of the one. It gave me a mighty feeling of loneliness, I can tell you, to see him doing these things. Finally, I said:

"I can't stay behind, Hugh."

He answered: "What sort of a man would I be, if I went in with a helper to fight against one man?"

I saw that I could not answer this with words, so I did not argue any more. We went off to get a meal, and then rented a small, damp, cold room, where we turned in.

I remember that Massey sat for a time on the edge of his bed with his chin in his hand.

"How far would Alec go?" he said over and over to himself. "How far would Alec go?"

"Clear back to nature," I said. "There was always about sixty percent wolf in him."

At this suggestion, he jerked back his head and groaned, but a moment later he wrapped himself in his blankets and went to sleep.

I was still dead tired from the trail when something waked me. I had heard nothing, but I had a definite feeling that I was alone in the room. A ghastly feeling in the arctic, and a thing that haunts many men on the trail—the dread that companions may leave them during the night.

I sat up with a jerk and, looking across the room, I could see by the dingy twilight that seeped through the little window that Massey had actually gone. He had gone for Pension Creek, of course, to get there and do his work before I arrived.

I jumped into my boots, and rolled my pack, and lighted out after him. I already had my sled in good order, after the division of the load. And the three dogs Massey had left for me were the better half of the pack. He was not the sort ever to give a friend the worst of anything.

In the cold bleakness of that morning, I got underway and headed out onto the Klondike. A low mist was hanging over the ice, over the town, over the trees. Breathing was difficult. I hated and dreaded the work before me and the goal to which I was driving, but I went on. I had been so long with Massey, thinking of his problems, and studying his welfare, and taking care of him, that I had no ability to attach myself to a lonely life and a goal of my own.

So I headed out there onto the ice.

It was very thin. Two or three times in the first mile I could feel it bending under me, and I increased the speed of the dogs for the sake of putting a less steady pressure upon any spot of the surface.

In this way I went over that first mile taking a zigzag course until I picked up the sign of a sled and dogs.

I studied the marks of the dog's feet, where the surface was soft enough to keep a clear print of them, and presently I came to the wide-spreading, three-toed impression of Bosh, the big sled dog. I knew that print well, and there was no doubt in my mind that it was Bosh, all right.

Then I noted the very marks that the sled left, and a certain slight tendency it had to side slip toward the right. By this I was confirmed in all that I had felt before. It was without mistake the lead sled of our outfit, and that was the team of Hugh Massey.

After this, I settled down to a rapid pace, pressing the dogs a little. They went extremely well, for they were not overloaded, and they seemed to know that they were heading after an old human friend and many dog companions.

The mist finally lifted and the way became brighter and easier. Finally, I could see Massey going along ahead of me, his dogs strung out and pulling hard. I smiled to myself as I watched the rhythm of his marching shoulders, for this was a place where a light weight

was better than a strong body. He had to go with con-
summate care over the frozen stream which had eaten
up one life so recently and, as he wove from side to
side, picking the secure going, and as his leader studied
the ice as a good dog should, he was losing ground and
time. I could march straight ahead without danger, and
well my wise leader knew it.

I could afford to slow up our pace. The steel runners
cut and gritted away at the cold road. The ice began to
glow with brilliant reflections, and sometimes we went
over places where the surface water had been frozen so
suddenly and strongly that it seemed to have been arrested in mid-leap—for it was still clear and translucent,
and every moment I expected to fall through the crust.

I stuck there in place behind my friend for several
hours, and still, to my amazement, he never turned his
head. Usually, he was as wary as a wild Indian, and he
could not go a mile without sweeping everything round
him with a glance.

But now it was a different matter. There was only one
point in the compass that had any meaning for him, and
this was the point toward which lay the claim of his
enemy, Calmont. As a matter of fact, I kept there behind
him, unnoticed, until he turned off the river to camp for
the night, and then I pulled up beside him.

You never could tell what Massey would do in such
a pinch as this. If he had ordered me furiously back to
Dawson, or berated me coldly for being a fool, or turned
a cold shoulder on me and said nothing at all, I should
not have been surprised.

Instead, he acted as though we had been marching
together all the day long and merely told me, quietly,
what I was to do in the work of preparing the camp.

We had about as cheerful a camp, that night, as we
ever had made. Of course, there was plenty of fuel, and

a whipping hail storm, followed by a fall of snow and then a gale of wind, was nothing to us. We ate a good big dinner, turned in, and slept just like rocks. At least, I can answer for my part.

In the morning, we resumed our march under a gray sky.

The wind had died before the snow stopped falling; the result was that the trees were streaked and piled with white along every branch, and now and then some unperceived touch of breeze would shake down a little shower, and make whispers of surprise in the forest. This snowfall dusted over the ice and gave a better grip for the dogs and, besides, it made the runners go more sweetly. For steel does not love ice, but bites hard upon it like a dog on a bone.

Our mileage was exceptionally good, this day, and we plugged along with a will. That night, Massey spoke for the first and last time about this new business I had taken in hand.

"I've tried to keep you out of this," he said, "and it seemed that I couldn't do it. Well, every man has to run his own business and, if you think that you belong here with me, perhaps you're right. You know, of course, that you're not to pull a gun on Calmont. I don't think that there'd be any need of it, anyway."

"Hugh," I said, "tell me how you feel about Calmont, really. Don't you sometimes remember that he was your old partner and bunkie?"

He looked thoughtfully aside at me, nodding his head at his own thought, and not at me.

"Sometimes at night," said Massey, "I dream of the old days. Yes, sometimes at night I remember him the way he used to be before he went mad. Why d'you ask?"

"Well, of course, I haven't been through what you

152

were through with him. Only, seeing that he was your old partner, I can't help wondering how...."

"How I could want to kill him?"

"Yes, that's it."

"It's horrible to you, I suppose?" he said.

"Yes, it's pretty horrible to me."

He nodded again, and even whistled a little, until I thought that his mind had wandered far away and left me. But at length he merely remarked: "Yes, I suppose it would seem that way to you."

This invitation of mine to have him talk a bit was not rewarded at all. But that good-natured calm of his reply, and the emotionless manner in which he received my suggestion of a conscience at work, meant more to me than if he had raved and gnashed his teeth and fallen into a stamping fury.

"Have you any doubt, Hugh?" I could not help going on.

"Doubt about what?" he said.

"About what will happen when you meet him? Are you sure that you can handle Calmont?"

He looked me straight in the eye and smiled.

"Just enough doubt, Joe," he said, "to make the business a lark."

Chapter Twenty-two
When Two Men Meet

When we reached Pension Creek, all the country was frozen as still as ice. The trees were like leaden clouds chained to the sides of the hills and frosted cold to the touch. It seemed that fire could never thaw and heat the iron hardness of that frozen wood. The axe edge I used bound back from it in my numb, weak fingers. The wind was iced into stillness, also, and for that we thanked our stars, because it was bitter weather even without a breeze to drive the invisible knife blades into us.

Never have I seen such evidences of cold, though I have no doubt that I have been in places where the thermometer sank lower. But here it was perhaps the dampness of the air which made every breath lodge, as it were, near the heart. The water seemed to have been checked in mid-flow, for instead of finding a solid, glassy surface, there were partial strata extending from the banks, turned to stone as they poured out on the main face of the water. This made very bumpy going. Besides, the stream was narrow, crooked, and had many cascades where we had to put all the dogs on one sled and heave with our shoulders to get it up.

It was a strange thing, that Pension Creek. Perhaps it was because we were drawing close to the claim where the battle was to be fought out, but it seemed to me that I never had seen a stream that wound in such a dark and secret snake trail through the woods.

We crawled with difficulty and pain up to the place where Pension Creek dwindled to a runlet.

"We should have taken the left fork," said Massey. "We've left the main stream."

I thought the same thing, but as we were about to check the dogs, we turned around a bend of the ice road and saw the shack before us. It was the usual thing— just a low log wall, with the look of crouching to avoid the cold. Close to the edge of the creek we saw the smudge of the thawing fire, and smoke was climbing out of the chimney at the end of the roof and walking up into the still air in a solid spiral. We stopped the team, then, swinging them close under the bank so that we could not be seen from the house.

Massey motioned to me to remain behind.

I wanted to. I had not the heart to see that battle but, on the other hand, I could not remain there shivering with the dogs, looking down at their heaving sides, when my friend was in that house fighting for his life. I wondered what it would be—a single crash and echo of an exploding gun, or a prolonged turmoil, a floundering struggle, perhaps someone yelling out, finally, as a knife or a bullet went home—perhaps only that awful noise which a choking man makes. I had heard that, once, during a rough-and-tumble fight in a Nome barroom.

Well, as Massey climbed up the bank, I climbed after him.

He was halfway toward the house when he knew I was coming. He paused and, glancing over his shoulder, shook his head and waved his hand to warn me back. But I would not be warned. He could not delay to argue the point. He went straight on, soft as a shadow, and I moved as silently as I could behind him.

This was as dreadful as anything that I ever have seen or heard of. I mean to say that stealthy, gliding motion with which Massey went toward the house, stalking a man.

He turned around the shoulder of the house just as the door squeaked in opening, and big Calmont walked out and fairly put his breast against the muzzle of Massey's revolver.

Massey was still crouching like a beast of prey. I looked to hear the shot and see Calmont fall dead but the calm of that big fellow was wonderful to see. He merely looked down at the gun and then leisurely turned his gaze upon Massey.

"Well, you got me," he said.

"Yes," said Massey. "I got you . . . boy!"

No cursing or berating, you see. It was worse than cursing, however; the deep satisfaction in Massey's voice. I can still hear it.

"Come in and sit down," said Calmont.

"Don't mind if I do," said Massey.

Calmont went in before us. He had fixed that door so that it closed with a spring, and it was an odd sight to watch him enter and hold the door open—as if he feared that the back-swing of the door might unsettle Massey's aim.

I pressed in behind them, and we sat down on three homemade stools, near the stove.

It was the sort of interior you would expect to find. Just naked usefulness and damp and misery. But this was made up for by the sight of some leather sacks in the corner of the room, lying unguarded on the floor. Two were plump. One was about half full.

"You've had luck," said Massey, and turned his head and nodded toward the pile of little sacks.

No doubt, in his mind was a hope that Calmont would be tempted by this turning of the head to pull a gun, if he wore one. And he did wear one. We learned afterward that even when he was sure that Massey would be blind forever, he could not live without a Colt constantly in his clothes or under his hand. No surety was enough to put Massey out of his mind and his fear.

However, this temptation was a little too patent and open. Calmont made no move toward drawing a weapon, but he answered: "Yes, I've struck it rich."

"That's good," answered Massey.

"Yeah. About thirty thousand dollars, if the stuff is seventeen an ounce."

"You've taken out near two thousand ounces?"

"Yeah. You see Sam Burr?"

"We saw him."

"How's Sam?"

"He's getting better. He's still a mite nervous."

"Yeah," said Calmont, "I reckon he might be. Never had nerves that were any good, Sam didn't."

He said to me: "There's some coffee in that pot, kid. Go fetch it and fill some cups. Honest coffee is what is there! There's some bacon yonder, too, and. . . ."

I got up.

"Sit still," ordered Massey. "We don't eat and we don't drink with Arnie Calmont."

The glance of Calmont a second time flickered from the gun up to the face of his old companion, and I knew what was in his mind. It was a clever move, too. The smell of that simmering coffee filled the room. My very heart ached for a long, hot draft of it; but; of course, when you eat and drink with a man in the North, you're bound to him as a guest, as he is to you as a host. This, among certain classes of men, is a sacred obligation. I could see at a glance where Calmont and Massey belonged in the category.

"Sam told you the way up?" said Calmont, not pressing his hospitality on us.

"No, he didn't," lied Massey.

Naturally, he did not want to draw the blame onto the head of any other man, or involve another in his quarrel.

"Nobody but Burr knew," said Calmont. "If they did, they'd be up here in a crowd . . . but Burr still hopes that he'll get out and manage to come up here and clean me out . . . and the rich surface deposits, too."

"You've gone and lost Alec," said Massey.

"Burr lost him," said Calmont.

"After you stole him," replied Massey.

"He's my dog," stated Calmont.

"He was judged to me."

"By that old fool, Borg."

"You swallowed his judgment."

"I swallowed nothing. A man has gotta back down when there's a dozen hired guns ready for him. But what Borg decided didn't make no difference to me."

"You agreed to it," said Massey.

"And what if I did? I never meant agreeing in my heart."

"No, that's your way," admitted Massey.

There was a good deal of sting in their words, but so far they had kept their voices gentle. This did not greatly surprise me in Massey. I knew him and the iron grip he kept on his nerves at all times. But it did surprise me in Calmont; there was so much brute in him.

He looked more the wolf than ever, now. His beard

and whiskers had been unshaved for a long time, and so his face was covered almost to the eyes with a dense growth, clipped off roughly and fairly short. Through this tangle his lips were a red line, and his eyes glittered.

This hair of Calmont's did not grow straight and orderly, as the hair of ordinary men grows, but it snarled and twisted a good deal like the coat of an Airedale, and increased his beast look a thousandfold. That, and the bright animal look in his little eyes.

I had only had, before, two good looks at him in all my life, but they had been on such occasions that the face of this man had been burned into my mind—a thing to dream of.

Now I looked at him partly as a human, and partly as a nightmare come true.

He did not pay much attention to me. Only now and then his glance wandered aside and touched on me. And I would rather have had vitriol trickled across my face. It was almost like having his big hands jump at my throat.

"That's my way," said Calmont, "and it's the right way. If ever there was a court of real law, what chance would you have agin' me, to claim Alec the Great?"

"The Alaska way is a good enough way for me," said Massey.

"Yeah? Well, we'll see."

"Very quick we'll see, too. This is gunna be decided forever, and right now!"

"All right," said Calmont, "it'll have to be decided, then."

To my amazement, he smiled a little, and this shocked me so much that I glanced quickly over my shoulder toward the door. It was closed, however. No silent partner of Calmont was standing there, to give him an unsuspected advantage. But, from the look on the man's face, you would have said that he had the upper hand, and that we were helpless before him.

"Are you wearing a gun?" said Massey.

"No," said Calmont.

"You lie," retorted Massey.

"Do I?"

"Yes. But we're going to see how long your lie will last. First of all, I want to chat with you for a few minutes."

"About sore eyes?" asked Calmont curiously.

At that temptation, I suspected that Massey would lose his self-control and murder the man straight off, but his shoulders merely twitched a little.

"About Alec," he said.

The lip of Calmont lifted like the disdainful lip of a wolf.

"I'll tell you nothin' about him!" he said.

Chapter Twenty-three
A Bargain Is Made

After this, Massey waited for a moment. Just how this odd duel between them was going to turn out, I could not guess.

"Put some wood into the stove," said Massey to me.

I did as he directed me, stepping around carefully so that I should not come between them. I put some wood into the stove and moved the damper so that the draft began to pull and hum up the chimney. Then I moved back where I could watch them both from the side. They were as different as could be, Calmont still with his snarling look, and Massey fixed and intent and staring. Wolf and bull terrier, one might say.

"You've lost Alec and you want him to stay lost?" queried Massey.

"That's my business," answered Calmont. "I'll gather him in when I want him. He's out to pasture."

"You know where he is, eh?"

"I know where he is," nodded Calmont.

Massey drew in a quick little gasping breath.

"Arnie," he said, "I've got you here in the hollow of my hand. But I'll give you another chance. I'll give you a free break for your gun. I'll put up this Colt and give you an equal break to get out yours."

"And how do I pay for the chance?" asked Calmont.

"It's free as can be. Tell me where to find Alec. Where he's running, I mean," answered Massey.

Calmont looked deliberately up to the ceiling, and then back at Massey. He was wearing the most disagreeable of sneers, as usual.

"I dunno that I'll do that," he said.

"What good would Alec be to you?" asked Massey calmly. "No matter if you know where he is. If he's running wild, you'll never catch him. He's too wise to be trapped. He's too fast to be caught by huskies; and he's too strong to be stopped by hounds. He's gone, as far as you're concerned."

"I'll take my chances," said Calmont sullenly.

"Even when you had him with you, what good was he to you, Arnie?"

"A dog don't have to do parlor tricks for me," answered Calmont in anger.

"You had to keep him muzzled. He hates you. What good is he to you, man?"

"The good of keepin' him away from you," answered Calmont. "You thief!"

"I'm a thief, am I?"

"Aye, and a rotten low one!"

"I've stolen what?"

"Alec, first. Then the girl. Then you sneaked away your own life through my hands, when I should've had you, and found you blind!"

His voice rose. He roared out the last words.

"I understand you," said Massey. "You're complaining of the way I've treated you. Did I ever try to murder you? Did I ever strike foul in a fight, as you did? Did I ever tie you hand and foot and leave you to starve or freeze to death without so much as a match near by to make a fire?''

''D'you think that I regret that?'' answered Calmont. ''No, I only wish that I'd been able to do what I wanted with you and leave you there to turn to ice.''

''You were a fool,'' said Massey. ''When the spring brought in the prospectors they would have been sure to find my body, and that would have meant hanging for you!''

''Would it? I'd be glad to hang, Massey, if I could send you out of life half a step ahead of me!''

I think that he meant what he said, there was such a brutal loathing in his face as he stared at Massey. Evil always seems more formidable than good, and I wondered that Massey dared to sit there and offer to fight Calmont on even terms.

''Let's get away from ourselves,'' said Massey, ''and talk about the dog. Alec . . . what earthly purpose have you in wanting that dog, man? He hates you. He has hated you nearly from the first.''

''You tricked him into it!'' declared Calmont.

''I? You had a fair chance at him, out there in that igloo. You know that you had a fair shot at him, Calmont!''

''You lie!'' said Calmont with the uttermost bitterness. ''You'd put your hands and your words onto him. How'd I have a chance? I couldn't talk dog talk, the way that you can! You tricked me out of my right in him!''

''You've had time since. What have you managed to do with him?''

''You think I've done nothin', eh?''

163

"Not a thing, I'd put my bet."

"Then you're a fool!" said Calmont. "It takes time. Time is all that I need with him. He's my dog, and down in his heart he knows that he's mine. He's like a sulky kid, that's all. But I can see through him. I know that he's mine at bottom and will be all mine, in a little time."

"He never so much as licked your hand!" said Massey.

"You lie!" shouted Calmont, in one of his furious rages. "He did when he was a pup, even."

"Before he was old enough to know better!"

"I tell you," shouted Calmont "that if it hadn't been for that fool Sam Burr, I would have had that dog talking my talk. I had to wait to let the rot you'd talked to him get out of his mind. But he was comin' my way. He was gunna be my dog ag'in. I tell you he ate out of my hand, the very mornin' of the last day that he was here!"

He cried this last out in a triumph. He was greatly excited. His eyes shone and his smile was like the smile of a child. All at a stroke, half of my fear and loathing of this man turned to pity. He had induced the dog actually to eat out of his hand, and this triumph still put a fire in his eyes! Yes, poor Calmont. He was simply not like other men.

"Tell me where he is," said Massey, "and you'll have an even break to polish me off. I'll put my gun on the ground. Then you can tell me!"

I saw Calmont measure the distance from the ground to Massey's hanging hand.

Then he shook his head.

"You're a trickster. You're a sleight-of-hander! Bah, Massey! D'you think that I've lived with you so long and don't know your ways?"

Massey waited, and watched him. Then, slowly and deliberately, he raised his revolver and covered the forehead of Calmont.

"I should have done it long ago," he said. "It's not a crime. It's a good thing to put a cur like you out of the world. You're a fiend. You're a cold-blooded snake, Calmont. You tried to murder me. Now I'm going to do justice on you."

"Hugh! Hugh!" I shouted. "It's murder!"

"Shut up and keep away from me!" said Massey, as cold as steel.

Calmont, in the meantime, did not beg for his life, did not flinch. I never hope to see such a thing again. He merely leaned a bit forward and looked with his usual sneering smile into the eye of the revolver, exactly like a man staring at a camera when his picture is about to be taken. His color did not alter. There was no fear in Arnold Calmont when he looked death in the face, and that is a thing worth remembering.

I saw the forefinger of Massey tighten on the trigger. He was actually beginning to squeeze it, with the slowness of a man who wants to prolong a pleasure as much as possible, and this time I ran in front of the gun.

It was a wild thing for me to do, but I was so excited that I forgot the gun might go off any second. I simply could not stand by and see such a frightful thing done. Yet I don't remember that there was a look of evil in the face of Massey. His attitude was that of an executioner. He detested Calmont so much that I think it was something like a holy rite—the slaughter of that wolf-faced man.

At any rate, I got in there between them on the jump and yelled out: "You'll never find Alec, if you shoot him! Alec will be gone for good, Hugh! Will you listen?"

I saw him wince. He snarled at me to get out of the way. But a moment later he stood up—it had been one of the chief horrors that these fellows were seated all through that talk, making the affair so utterly casual. Then he said: "You're right! Why should I throw away my chances at Alec for the sake of butchering this animal? Step away, son. I won't pull the trigger."

He dropped the gun to his side as he spoke, and I sidestepped gladly from between them.

What immediately followed, I only vaguely know, because the instant the excitement was over, my knees fairly sagged under me. I had a violent sense of nausea, and dropping down on a stool, I held my head in both hands. There is shock from a punch or a fall; there is a worse shock from mere horror, and every nerve in me felt this one.

I remember that Massey finally said: "Calmont, there's no good throwing away a great thing because we hate each other. We both want that dog. If you won't tell me where he is, come along with me and we'll hunt him together. The man who gets him, turns him in to the fund, so to speak, and then we'll fight it out for that. You don't think you're quite my size with a gun. Then we'll have it out with bare hands, if you want. How does that sound to you?"

I groaned a little as I thought of this possibility. The two of them, I mean, turned into beasts and tearing and beating at one another.

"We hunt for Alec first and, when we've got him, we fight for him? Is that it?" asked Calmont, with a new ring in his voice.

"Aye, that's it."

"Massey," said the wolf man, "there's something in you, after all. You got brains. I'll shake with you on that!"

166

"I'd rather handle a rattler," said Massey.

"Dang you!" burst out Calmont. "I'll choke better words than that out of you, before the end!"

They glared at each other like wild animals for a moment, but there were bars between them now—that is to say, they were kept from murder on the spot by the knowledge that they needed one another. There was such a gigantic will in each of them that I felt thin and light as an autumn leaf, helped up in the air by the pressure of adverse winds.

"Cut some bacon," said Massey to me.

I went to do it. My knees were still sagging under me, and my hand shook when it grasped the knife, but I was eager to have this accomplished. I got that bacon sliced into the pan in short order, and when it was cooked and the flapjacks frying afterward, then I laid it on tin plates and served coffee.

They each picked up some bacon and a cup of the coffee at the same time, and at the same instant they were about to drink, when I saw their eyes meet and their hands lower. Each had the same thought, I suppose, that if they ate and drank together in this manner, then it would be necessary for them religiously to respect the truce until Alec was taken.

Then they drank at the same instant, watching each other fiercely above the rims of the cups.

For my part, I made a prayer that Alec should never be caught.

Chapter Twenty-four
Honors Are Even

It is by no means an unusual thing for men to fall out in the North and still to continue in a form of partnership, for the mere good reason that man power is worth something up there in the frozen land. You will see partners together who really hate one another for everything except muscle worth. But that was very different from the way of Calmont and Massey, now that they were together.

Their hatred was so uniquely perfect that sometimes I had to rub my eyes and stare at them. I could not realize that they were there before me, one of them making trail, and one of them driving the dogs and working the gee pole. But one thing I found out at once—that they traveled like the wind.

Calmont had no dogs at all. They had been either run off or killed by wolves, he said; and, when he admitted this, Massey had grown suddenly thoughtful.

"Your dogs were all run off before Alec left?" he asked.

"No. After," said Calmont.

"And what about the wolves?"

"I know what you mean," said Calmont gloomily.

"Well, d'you think that it's right?"

"He's gone wild," said Calmont. "There ain't any doubt of that. I know that he's gone wild and that it'll be the dickens to get him back. There's a lot of wolf blood in him, Hugh. You know that. His ma was mighty treacherous before him."

"You think that he's gone back to some wolf tribe, Arnie?"

"I reckon he has. Or else he's leadin' those four huskies of mine and getting them back to the wild. Any way you figger it, he's gone."

"What makes you think you know where to find him?"

"There come in an Injun here one day, and he talks to me a little while he eats my chow. He's seen a white wolf, he tells me."

"Alec?"

"Alec sure!"

"Where did he see him?"

"A good long march over the ridge."

"And how did he see him?"

"He was out with a pair of dogs, and goin' along pretty good one day when he come to dark woods and while he was in the thick of the shadow of 'em, out comes a rush of wolves, with a big white one in the front, and those murderin' brutes they killed and half ate his dogs right under his eyes."

"That doesn't sound like Alec!"

"He ain't the same!" said the other. "When Alec was

169

with you, he was only a pup. But now he's grown up,
and he's growed bad . . . in spots. The wolf in him has
come out a good deal lately!''

He suddenly saw that this, in a very definite sense,
was a criticism of himself, and he bit his lip. Wherever
Alec was concerned he was as thin-skinned as a girl,
though in all other matters he was armored like a rhi-
noceros.

"Did this white wolf have Alec's marking?"

"He had black ears."

"No black on his muzzle and tail tip?"

"His muzzle was red by the time that Injun got a fair
look at it, and I reckon that Alec was moving so fast
that his tail tip couldn't be seen very clearly."

"There've been white wolves before, and even white
wolves with black ears. What makes you think that this
was Alec?''

"Well, I'll tell you that, too. The Injun said that one
of the wolves behind the white leader had a long strip
of gray down its right shoulder, and a squarish head for
a wolf, and by the rest of that description I made out a
pretty good picture of Bluff, my sled dog. So I figgered
that the band of wolves that jumped that outfit was simply Alec and my team behind him, runnin' wild."

Massey, at this, considered for a moment.

"And you're heading now for the place where those
wolves were seen?"

"No, I sent that Injun back on good, fat pay, to trail
that pack and find out what he could about it. He went
off with his one-dog sled, and he came back without it.
He said that after he got over that ridge, he had been
tackled in the middle of the night by the same pack, and
that he himself had seen the white leader cut the throat
of his one dog as if with a knife. He was pretty excited,
that Injun, when he came back here. He wanted most of

the world, to pay him back for that sled and the dog that he had lost.''

"You gave him some cash, I suppose," said Massey.

"Yeah, I give him some cash to square himself, for one thing."

Suddenly, Massey grinned.

"And you gave him a licking for the rest of what he wanted?''

Calmont grinned in turn.

"You know me pretty good, Hugh," he said.

I saw them smiling at one another with a perfect though mute understanding, and for the first time since I had met Massey, and heard of Calmont, I saw how these two men might have been companions and bunkies for years together, as every one knew they had been.

Massey turned off this familiar and friendly strain to say: "Look here, Calmont. Maybe they're five hundred miles from where you saw them.''

"You know wolves, do you?" asked Calmont, in his usual snarling voice.

"Pretty well.''

"You don't know a dang thing about 'em! A wolf don't usually run on more than a forty-mile range. And likely even the winter starving time won't make him wander more than a hundred, or so. They gotta have the knowledge of the country that they run in, or they're pretty nigh afraid even to hunt. Like Eskimo, you might say.''

"Why like Eskimo?''

"Well, I recollect bein' up north on the borders of the Smith Bay, I think it was, and I had some Eskimos along with me, and we was winterin' there, and I told 'em to put out their fish nets and try to catch something. But they said that there wasn't no fish in them waters, and that there wasn't any use in wastin' time on them.

171

And then along comes a bunch of the native tribe that knows that shore, and they put out their nets and catch a ton of fish, and we all ate them. After that, my Eskimos wanted to stay there forever, but I had to move. Well, wild animals are the same way. They hunt in the country that they know.''

''But Alec never knew any wild country.''

''He'll learn to, then. And within a coupla days' marches of where that Injun found him and the dog team that he swiped, we'll have a pretty fair shot to find him, too.''

Massey, after a time, admitted that this was true, and that was the reason that we kept on toward the place.

Of course, it would seem madness to most people, but not to me. I had seen Alec. This amount of trouble, no dog was really worth; but Alec was not a dog. A wolf, then, you ask? No, not a wolf, either. But he had learned so much from Massey that, when I saw him, he was almost half human.

To see that dog bringing his master matches, or gun, or slippers, or parka, well, it was worth a good deal. To see him walk a tightrope was a caution, and to see a thousand other ways that he had of acting up was a caution too. The only way that Massey punished him was, when he had been really bad, to leave him outside of the tent at night. And there Alec would sit and cry like a baby and mourn like a wolf, until finally he was let in.

Outside of that, I never had seen Massey so much as speak rough to him, far less strike him with hand or whip. They were partners, as surely as ever man and man were partners. Why, for my own part, I never had much influence with Alec. I was not what you would call an intimate acquaintance, but still it gripped my heart like a strong hand when I thought of him being lost to us and condemned to the wilderness, where no man would ever again see the bright, fierce, wise, affectionate eyes.

Yes, in my own way I loved Alec, though it is hard for a boy to give his heart as freely as a man does. Boys are more selfish, more impulsive, more womanish than grown men. They make a fuss about an animal, or a person. But here were two grown men—the hardest I have ever known—who were willing to die for the sake of getting that dog back in traces!

This taught me a good deal. I used to watch the pair of them, day after day. The wonder of this situation never left me, but all the while I was saying to myself that they were laboring together like brothers for a goal which, when they reached it, would make them kill one another.

It was the strangest thing that I ever saw. It was the strangest thing that ever was imagined. But they needed one another. Calmont could not catch the dog without the help of Massey, and Massey could not find the region where Alec was ranging without the help of Calmont. There they were, loathing one another, but tied to each other by a common need.

I can tell you two strange things that happened on that out-trail.

The third day we came to a place where the surface ice suddenly thinned—I don't know why, on that little mangy stream—but Massey, who was making trail, suddenly broke through and disappeared before our eyes.

I say that he disappeared. I mean that he almost did but, while one of his hands was still reaching for the edge of the ice and breaking it away, Calmont with a yell threw himself forward and skidded along on hands and legs, like a seal—to keep the weight over a bigger surface—until he got to the edge of the hole in a mo-

173

ment, and caught the hand of Massey just as it was taking its last hold.

When he tried to pull Massey out, the ice gave way in great sections, and I think they would have gone down together, if I hadn't swerved the team away from the place and thrown Calmont a line.

By the aid of that, and the dogs and I pulling like sixty, we got them both out on the ice, and I started a huge fire, and they were soon thawing out.

But the wonderful part was not so much the speed with which Calmont had gone to the rescue, as it was his bulldog persistence in sticking to the rescue work in spite of the fact that every instant it looked as though the powerful current would pull down both the drowning man and the would-be rescuer.

This amazed them both, also, I have no doubt. But the point of the matter was that no thanks were given or expected. They growled at each other more than ever, and seemed ashamed.

The very next day, we were going up a steep, icy slope. When Calmont, ahead of us, slipped and fell like a stone, I got out of the way with a yell of fear, but Massey stood there on the ledge of frozen, slippery rock, with a fifty-foot drop just behind him. To see the last of Calmont, he only needed to step out of the way, but he wouldn't. He tackled that spinning, falling body. The shock of it dragged them both to the trembling brink of the drop, but there they luckily lodged, two inches from death for them both.

They simply got up and shook themselves like dogs, and went on with the day's march.

Chapter Twenty-five
The Moose

That same night, when we camped, I watched the pair of them carefully, for I had high hopes that murder might no longer be in the air. There is no greater thing a man may do than lay down his life for a friend. And if that is true, what is to be said of him who has offered to lay down his life?

Well, each of these man had done exactly that for the other. But instead of a thawing of that cold ice of hatred which encased them both, they looked at one another, so far as I could tell, with an increased aversion. It was perfectly clear to me that what they had done was simply for the sake of forwarding the march; for the sake of Alec the Great, you might say. And that seemed more and more true as I stared at them.

They never spoke to one another, if they could avoid it. Often when something had to be said, one of them would speak to me, so that he could make his mind clear on a subject. This may seem childish, but it did not strike me that way. There was too much danger in the air.

The night settled down on us damp and thick with cold. A really deadly mist poured into the hollows and rose among the trees until we could see only the ones near at hand. And even those looked like ghosts waiting around us. So we built up a whacking big fire to drive away the cold, and in this way we made ourselves fairly comfortable, though comfort is only a comparative thing that far north. Sometimes I found myself wishing for the fireless camps of the open tundra in preference to this choking mist which lay heavy on the lungs with every breath that we drew.

I tried to make a little talk as we sat around the fire, getting the ache of the march out of our legs, but they stared at the flames, or at one another, and they would not answer me except with grunts. They were thinking about the future, and Alec, and the fight that was to come, no doubt, and they could not be bothered by the chatter of a youngster like me.

We all turned in, with a fire built up on each side, and a tunnel of warmth in between. That is an extravagant way of camping, because it takes so much wood chopping, but we had three pairs of hands for all work and we could afford to waste wood and a little labor.

In the middle of the night, I sat up straight, with my heart beating and terror gripping me, for I had just had a dream in which Calmont had leaned over me with his wolfish face and, opening his mouth, showed me a set of real wolf's fangs to tear at my throat.

Naturally I stared across at him, and there I saw him, sitting up as I was, and his face more wolfish than ever in that reddish half light. For the fire had died down, throwing up a good deal of heat, but only enough light to stain the deathly mist that had crept in close about the camp. Through this fog I saw Calmont watching me, and the shock was even worse than the nightmare.

He lifted his head as though listening to something. Then, far away, I heard the cry of wolves upon a blood trail. At least, so it sounded to me, for I always feel that I can recognize the wolf's hunting cry. And certainly the sound was traveling rapidly across the hills, dipping dimly into valleys and rising loud on the ridges. Massey jumped up at that moment. The sight of him was as good as a warm sunrise to me. He made my blood run smoothly again.

"That may be the pack we're after," said Massey.

We threw on the fire enough wood to scare away wild animals, and then we struck out on a line that promised to cut the path of the wolves, if they held a straight course.

A few paces from the fire, the mist closed thickly over us; but when we got to the first ridge, a wind struck the fog away, or sent it in tangles through the trees. We had been stumbling blindly, before, but now we had a much better light.

Calmont held up a hand to order a halt, and listened. In such moments he was the natural master, for he was a good woodsman. Massey looked to him and mutely accepted his leadership.

"The hill!" said Calmont, and started down the slope at a great speed, nursing his rifle under the pit of his arm.

We crossed the hollow, slipping on the ice that crusted the frozen stream there, and toiled up the farther slope to the next crest. There Calmont put us in hiding in the brush, at a point where we could look down on a considerable prospect.

Ice encased the naked branches and the slender stems of the brush. The cold of it brushed through my clothes and set me shivering, while we listened to the pack as it swung over a height, dropped into a vagueness in a hollow, and again boomed loudly just before us.

We were about to see something worth seeing, and perhaps it was the ghostliness of the night, the strange arctic light, the still stranger mist in the trees, that made me feel very hollow and homesick, so that with a great pang I wished myself back among the Arizona sands, and the smoky herbage of the desert. This scene was too unearthly for my taste.

"They're running fast," said Massey, canting his ear to the noise.

"Shut up!" answered Calmont in his usual growl.

And Massey was still. In the woods, he always acknowledged Calmont's leadership.

Over the ridge before us now broke the silhouette of a great bull moose, and he came down the slope with enormous strides. He looked like a mountain of meat, loftier than the stunted trees, and streaking behind him, gaining at his heels, was a white wolf.

All snow-white he looked in that light, a beautiful thing to watch as he galloped.

"Alec!" said Massey under his breath.

And suddenly I knew that he was right. Yes, and now I could see, I thought, the black ears and tail tip, and the dark of Alec's muzzle. But he looked twice as big as when I last had seen him.

How my heart leaped then! Not only to see him, but to realize that this was the goal toward which we had traveled so far, and that for the sake of Alec even such enemies as Calmont and Massey had sworn a truce. To avoid the battle that would surely come after his capture, suddenly I wished that the big hoofs of the moose would split the skull of Alec to the brain. I mean that I almost wished this, but not quite; for to wish for Alec's death was almost like wishing for the death of a man, he had such brains and spirit, and a sort of human resolute courage.

Behind Alec, over the rim of the ridge, pitched four more running, and Calmont immediately exclaimed: "My team! Mine and maybe the Injun's dog!"

Well, they looked wolfish enough, except that one had a white breast plate that no wolf was apt to show. They seemed half dead from running, but they kept on, with Alec showing them the way to hold on to a trail.

In the flat of the hollow the moose hit a streak of ice, floundered, and almost fell. He recovered himself, but the effort seemed to take the last of his wind and strength, for instead of bolting straightway, he whirled about and struck at Alec with a forehoof. It was like the reach of a long straight left, and it would have punched Alec into kingdom come if it should have landed.

Well, it did not land. I suppose that at such a time the training Alec had had in dodging whip strokes stood him in good stead. Even the lightning stroke of a bull moose is not so fast as the flick of a whiplash.

The moose was well at bay, now, as Alec swerved from the blow. The other huskies came up with a rush, but they did not charge home. They knew perfectly well that there was death in any stroke from that towering brute. So they sat down in the snow and hung out their tongues. They moved, however, to different points of the compass. No one could have taught them much about moose hunting. But here was where the wolf blood, in which they were rich, came to their help. They maneuvered so that they could threaten the moose from any side; and he, with constant turnings of his head, marked them down with his little, bright eyes.

While the four sat down at the four points of the compass, as it were, Alec stalked around as chief inspector and director of attack.

Calmont pulled his rifle to his shoulder. But Massey jerked it down

"He'll train Alec!" protested Calmont.

"Never in the world!" declared Massey. "That dog can take care of himself against anything but a thunderbolt, and even a lightning flash would have to be a real bulls-eye to hit that dodging youngster. No, no, Arnie! We've got to use this chance to work down close to him. Move softly. They've got something on their hands now that'll make their ears slow to hear, but anything is likely to put them on the run. They've gone wild, Arnie. They've gone wild, and Heaven knows whether or not Alec is too wild ever to be tamed again! Let's sneak down on them, men. I want to get close enough so that he can hear my voice well enough to know it. That's our one chance, I take it!"

Calmont did not protest. What Massey said seemed too thoroughly right to be argued against, and therefore we all began to work down the slope through the verge of the brush.

Mind you, this was a frightfully slow business. The frozen twigs of the bushes were as brittle as glass and as likely to snap. And, as Massey had said, the least alarm might send these wild ones scampering. We had to mind every step, everything against which we brushed, putting back the little branches as cautiously as though they were made of diamonds.

What I saw of the scene in the hollow was somewhat veiled, naturally, by the branches that came between me and the moving figures, but nothing of importance escaped me, because I was breathlessly hanging on the scene.

That moose looked as big as an elephant, and the wolves shrank into insignificance in comparison. However, the man-trained dog, Alec, went calmly about, prospecting. It looked exactly as though he were laying out a plan of attack, and a moment later we could see what was in his mind. I suppose that animals can only communicate with one another in a vague way, but it appeared exactly as though Alec had done some talking.

The next moment the attack was neatly made. All the wolves rose to their feet at the same moment—wolves, I say, for wolves they were now!—and as the moose jumped a bit with excitement, Alec made straight for his head.

It was only a feint. He merely made a pretense of driving in for the throat, though he came so close in this daring work that he had to squat, as the moose hit like a flash over his head. Then, as he leaped back, the second half of the attack went home. For a big husky sprang at the moose from behind and tried for the hamstring with gaping mouth.

He had delayed too long. He had not quite timed his attack with the feint of the boss. The result was that the moose had time to meet the second half of the battle with a hard-driven kick.

The wolf sailed far off through the air with a death shriek that rang terribly through the hollow and so ended the first phase of the contest.

Chapter Twenty-six
Alec, the Fighter

We were down a bit nearer, when the second half of the battle actually began. After the death of the first husky, the others showed a strong mind to go on their way; this mountain of meat suddenly smelled rank in their nostrils, for they had made a clever attack, and they had gained nothing but a dead companion.

Calmont was very angry. They had looked on while one of his dogs was killed, and the thing rubbed him the wrong way.

However, Massey convinced him that we would have to be more patient, and we were. We went on working our way closer and closer down the slope, keeping well into our screen of brush. For the dogs, after all, did not draw off. They had only four, altogether, by this time, and four looked like a small number to beat that wise and dangerous old fighter, the moose.

Alec, however, continued to walk around his circle, and he seemed to force his friends to get in closer—up to the firing line, as you might say, from which a quick rush and leap would get them to the enemy.

I suppose the moose felt that the game was in his hands, by this time, but he maintained a perfect watch and ward.

I noticed everything that followed very closely, for I was in an excellent position, and the detailed maneuvering was as follows:

One of the huskies worked around until he was exactly in front of the head of the big quarry. Two others took positions on the sides. Alec, in the meantime, in one of his slow circles, came just behind the heels of the moose.

This was the time agreed upon. You would have thought that, having failed in these tactics the first time, Alec would not try them again. There are other ways of bothering a moose, but perhaps Alec felt that there was none so good as this. On this occasion, the husky in front made the feint at the head. He was not so sure of himself as Alec had been. Or, perhaps, he was discouraged by the poor success of the first venture. At any rate, he only made a feeble feint, which caused the moose to lift a forefoot, without striking.

However, the rear attack was in better hands—or perhaps I should say feet and teeth. At the precise moment when the husky made his clumsy and half-hearted feint, Alec sprang in like a white flash. I saw the gleam of his big fangs, and I could almost hear the shock of the stroke as his teeth struck the hamstring full and fair, as it seemed to me.

Then he dropped flat to the ground, and the moose, with the uninjured leg, kicked twice, like lightning, above the head of Alec. After that, the dog jumped back like a good boxer who has made his point and lets the judges note it.

The stroke had gone home, but it had not cut the cord in two. The big beast still was standing without a sign of failing on any leg, and though he shook his head, he seemed as formidable and unhurt as ever.

That touch of the spur at least made him restless. While Alec licked his red-stained lips, and the other dogs stood up, trembling with fresh hope and fresh hunger, the quarry wheeled and fled with his long-striding trot. After him went the pack, but not far. For though the stroke of Alec had not quite severed the cord, it must have been hanging together by a mere thread. I could almost swear that I heard a distinct sound of something parting under high tension, and the moose slipped down on his haunches, sliding on the icy crust of the snow and knocking up a shower of it before him.

That slip was the last of him, and again Alec was the operator—or swordsman. He whipped around under the head of that big fighter and cut his throat for him as well as any butcher could have done. Then back he jumped.

The moose tried to rise. He floundered and fell again with a dog hanging to either flank, tearing, and Alec's teeth again slashed his throat. That was almost the finishing stroke.

My hair stood up on my head. There was something unbelievably horrible about this. It was like seeing three or four kindergarten children pull down a gigantic athlete and pommel him to death! All in a moment the moose was down, and dead, and the pack was eating.

But then I saw the explanation, and the horror left me. It was brains that had won. Alec, like a general overlooking a battlefield, stood up with his forefeet on the head of the moose and looked over his friends and their feasting with a red laugh of triumph—a silent laugh, of course, but one whose meaning you could not mistake.

He was the fellow with the brains. He was steel

against stone; powder against bow and arrows; science against brute power. The very fact that he restrained his appetite now was the proof that he had a will and a power of forethought.

I had seen him before a great deal. He had shown me more favor than to any one outside of his master, Massey. But, nevertheless, I never before had guessed what a great animal he was, and why two men were willing to risk their lives to get him. I knew now, fully, as I watched him standing over the head of his kill.

He had broadened and strengthened in appearance. I had last seen him as half a puppy; but now he was the finished product, and this life in the open, I could guess, and the starvation periods, and the interminable trails, and the hard battles, were the things which had tempered and hardened his fine metal to just the cutting edge.

I heard Calmont muttering softly to himself. His eyes blazed; his face was working. I suppose he would have given almost anything in the world to possess Alec, just then. Massey, however, to whom the dog meant still more, said not a word to anyone, but continued to work softly, delicately, through the brush.

We were not the only creatures who were stealing up on the feasting huskies, however. Alec the Great had not yet tasted the first reward of his victory, when out of the brush on the farther side of the hollow streamed five timber wolves.

You could tell the difference instantly between them and the huskies. They were tall, but slighter. Their tails were more bushy. There was more spring in their stride, and by the flat look in their sides and the movement of the loose robe over their shoulders, it was fairly certain that they were burned out with starvation. A dog, as thin as that, would hardly have been able to walk. It would have lain down to let the cold finish what starvation had almost ended. But a wolf keeps its strength and endurance almost as long as it can stand.

These five came on with a rush, forming a flying wedge, with the big gray leader in front. Calmont would have unhesitatingly used his gun at once, and I was of the same mind, but again Massey protested.

"You'll see something," he said, "if those dogs have rubbed off the man smell in the woods and the snow."

Afterward, I understood what he meant.

At the first sound behind him, Alec gave the snarl that was the danger signal and, at the sound of it, as he whirled about, the three who followed his orders leaped up beside him and presented a solid front to the foe.

They looked big enough and strong enough to do the trick, but I knew that they could not. There's only about one dog in a thousand that can fight a wolf single-handed. Even a half-bred husky, bigger, stronger in every other way, lacks the jaw power which is the wolf's distinguishing virtue. The house dog has no chance at all. Back in Arizona, I had seen a single lobo, and not a big one at that, fight three powerful dogs. He killed one of them with a single stroke. And he was slashing the others to bits when I managed to get a lump of lead into his wise and savage brain.

Alec was a different matter. He was man-trained before he ever began to learn the lessons of the wilderness and, after seeing what he had done to the moose, I should not have been surprised if he could take care of himself with a single wolf of average powers. However, I did not think that his company would last long against that savage assault. It would be soon over, and the wild wolves would sweep on to the moose meat that waited before them.

That was why I stared at Massey, who was dragging down Calmont's rifle for the second time.

Then I saw Alec do a strange thing that took my breath.

He left the moose; he left his three companions, and walked a few stiff-legged steps straight out to meet the enemy.

I thought at first that he meant to take the whole first brunt on himself, which would have meant a quick death.

That was not the meaning of it, however. The finesse of arctic etiquette, at least among wolves, was not yet familiar to me.

As soon as Alec went out there by himself, the rush of the wolf pack was stayed. Four of them finally stopped short and stood in a loose semicircle, their red tongues hanging out, and their little eyes fiery bright. Their whole charge from the brush had had a queer effect which I am not able to describe. It was as though some of the mist tangles in the trees had taken on solid weight and life, and had come out there with feet and teeth.

This was a serious matter. I wondered how far those dogs and wolves would have to travel to find another meat mountain like that moose? It was as though a small crew of buccaneers had captured a towering galleon laden with gold and spices, and had been surprised while plundering by a greater crew of pirates.

Now that the wolves had halted in their charge, I began to see how the thing might work out.

The leader, after giving a glance to right and left at his rank and file, stalked out by himself toward Alec. They came straight on toward one another until they were no more than six steps apart. There they paused, in different attitudes.

The wolf dropped his head; his hair bristled along his back; his hanging brush almost touched the ground; and his face had the most wicked expression. Alec, on the other hand, kept his head up, and there was no sign of bristling fur. He was on watch, I would have said; and he needed to be, for that timber wolf went at him in a moment like the jump of an unfastened spring.

"Watch!" said Massey.

It was worth watching. Since then, I've seen a burly prize fighter rush wildly at a smaller foe and be knocked kicking at the first blow. Alec was not so tall, but he was heavier than his wild brute, and he had man-trained brains. Wolf fighting is leap, stroke, shoulder blow or shoulder parry, and always a play to knock the other off his feet.

Well, Alec stood up there like a foolish statue while that gray wolf bolt flew at him across the snow, silent and terrible. At the very moment of impact, Alexander the Great dropped flat to the ground and reached for the other's throat with his long jaws. They spun over and over, but at the end of the last gyration, the wolf leader lay on his back, and Alec stood over him, slowly and comfortably crushing the life out at his throat!

Chapter Twenty-seven
Wild Blood

No fight to the death is a pretty thing to watch. The way Alec set his teeth, like a bulldog, while the gray leader kicked and choked and lolled his red tongue, made me more than a bit sick. However, the other wolves and the rest of the dogs did nothing about it. They had not moved from their places, which made a rough circle, except for an old wolf bitch who ran up while the struggle was going on and trotted around and around the two warriors, sometimes whining, once sitting down on her haunches, and howling at the sky.

I wondered whether she were the wife or the mother of the big gray wolf. Certainly he seemed to mean something to her, but she did not bare a tooth to help him in this pinch. A mysterious law of the wilderness made her keep hands off religiously during the battle.

It was over in just a minute. Alec stood back from the dead body of his enemy and, crouched a bit, with his back fur rising, he sent up a howl that filled me full of cold pins and needles. Even Massey groaned faintly as we heard this yell.

This ghoulish howl of triumph ended before any of the huskies or the wolves stirred; but when it was over the whole gang threw themselves on the moose and made a red riot of that good flesh. Alec went in to get his share now, also, and in less time than one could imagine, those powerful brutes were gorging in the vitals of the big carcass.

"He's run amok," said Massey through his teeth, very softly. But he was so close to me that I heard every word. "He's gone back to his wild blood! I'll never get him, now!"

That was exactly how I felt about it, too. It looked as though big Alec were the purest wolf in the world, and one of the biggest. He had seemed to loom among the huskies, but he looked still bigger compared to the wild beasts. He was in magnificent condition. Even in that dim light, there was a sheen in his long, silky coat, and that is a sure sign of health in a dog.

Well, I watched Alec in there getting his meal and told myself that there was mighty little similarity between him and the dog I had known. The color and marking were the same, and that was all. The whole air of him was different. This wild, grim Alexander the Great looked up to his name, more than ever, but I was sure that I wanted nothing to do with him, until I had been properly introduced to him all over again by Massey.

Massey himself had led the way down to the edge of the brush which was closest to the kill and the feasters. Then he turned his head to us and warned us with a gesture to keep back out of sight and to make no noise. The look with which he accompanied that silent warning was something to remember for a long time, it was so frightened, and so tense. A man might look just like that before he asked the lady of his heart to marry him.

Then out into the open stepped Massey.

At the sight of him, the old female who had made the fuss about the fight leaped right straight up into the air with a warning yip. Her back had been turned fairly on us, but she was apparently one of those vixens who have eyes wherever they have nerves. This warning of hers whipped the rest of the lot away from the moose. They scattered like dead leaves in a wind, for a short distance, and then they swirled about and faced us.

Only Alec stood his ground in the grandest style, facing Massey, with his forepaws on the shoulder of the moose, and his muzzle and breast crimsoned. There he waited, wrinkling his lips in rage and hatred as he saw the man step out from the brush. A good picture he made just then—a good picture to scare a tiger with.

Massey walked out slowly, but not stealthily. He held out one hand and said in a perfectly natural voice—or perhaps there was just a shade of quiver in it—"Hello, Alec, old boy!"

Alec went up in the air as the old wolf had done before him. You would have thought that there was dynamite in the words of his master. He landed a bit back from the head of the moose while the other huskies and the wolves took this for a signal, and scattered into the shadows and mists of the opposite line of brush.

"Alec!" called Massey again, walking straight on with his hand extended.

Alexander the Great spun around and bolted for the brush, with his ears flattened and his tail tucked between his legs.

Great Scott, how my heart beat! There was the end, I thought, of Alec the Great, the thinking dog, the king of his kind. He would be a king of the woods, now, in exchange for his former position. I don't suppose that the change could be called a step down, from his own viewpoint.

"Alec, Alec!" called Massey, in a sort of agony.

But Alec went out of sight among the brush with a rush of speed.

Massey ran forward, stumbling, so that it was pretty certain he was more than half blind. Poor Massey! He called again and again.

But I heard big Calmont gritting his teeth, and I felt, also, that it was a lost cause, when, out of the shadows popped that white beauty in the black mask and stood not twenty steps from Massey.

"Thank God!" I distinctly heard Massey say.

Then he went toward Alec carefully, hand out in the usual, time-honored gesture. And finally Alec made a defiant response.

He did not bolt this time. Instead, he dropped to his belly, and looked for all the world as though he were on the verge of charging straight at the man. He had all the aspects of a dog enraged and ready for battle, not for flight.

He looked more evil than he had when he was at the torn body of the moose, warning the man away.

However, when he rose it was not to charge.

He got up slowly, and I saw that the ruff of stiffened mane no longer stood out around his neck and shoulders. He stopped the snarling which had been rumbling in the hollow of his body like a furious and distant thunder. A sort of intimate thunder, one might say. And strung out straight and still, like a setter on a point, he poked his nose out at Massey and seemed to be studying the man.

It was as though he were half statue and half enchanted.

"He's gunna win," said Calmont thorough his teeth.

"He's got him charmed like a snake charms a bird!"

He was glad to see Massey show such a power over the dog, of course; but just the same, he could not help hating the man for the very strength which he showed. I believe that Calmont, in his heart, was profoundly convinced that Massey possessed the evil eye which masters beast and man.

In the meantime, Massey stopped advancing, and continued to talk gently and steadily to the dog. Alec lost his frozen pose and came up to his master, one halting step after another, exactly as though he were being pulled on a rope. Calmont began to swear softly under his breath.

Alec was about a stride away from the outstretched hand of his man, and I looked to see him ours in another instant, but then a very odd trick of fate turned up. In the woods, close at hand, a wolf howled sharp and thin. I don't know why, but I was instantly convinced that it was the old female wolf.

At her call, Alec twitched around and was gone in a gleaming streak across the clearing and into the wood toward the voice.

So the victory was snatched out of the very fingertips of Massey! And that wolf cry out of the mist of the forest was the most uncanny part of a very uncanny night.

Massey did not wait there any longer. He turned about and called us out, for he said that Alec would not come back again, that night.

"Or any other night!" said Calmont. "He's gone for good!"

Massey did not answer, except with a look that cut as deep as a knife stroke.

We set about cutting up the moose, slashing away the parts which the wolves and dogs had mangled, and finding, of course, a vast plenty that had not been spoiled. Everything would be good, either for us or for our team! It was a mountain of meat, for sure.

I was sent back to the camp to hitch up the team to an empty sled and bring it back, so that the meat could be loaded on board, since there was far more than three back loads in the heap, naturally. So I went off, with the howling of the wolves, as it seemed to me, floating out at me everywhere, from the horizon of the circling hills.

When I got near the site of our camp, I rubbed my eyes, amazed. For there was no sign of the tent. It had vanished!

Yet it was certainly our site. For presently I recognized the cutting in the adjacent grove, and then, hurrying on closer, I saw the explanation. The tent was there, but it had been knocked flat to the ground, while the snow all about was trampled and scuffed a lot.

Just before the tent lay the body of Muley, one of the poorer dogs in the team of Massey. He had had his throat cut for him neatly, after the wolf style, and somehow I could not but suspect that Alec the Great had done the job. It looked his style of things.

The other five dogs were gone, and I knew where. It was pretty plain to me that Alec was an organizing genius. The way he had mastered both half-wild huskies and all the wild timber wolves was a caution, and I could swear that he had stormed along on our back trail until he found our camp; and then, after corrupting the minds of the dog team with a few insidious whispers about the pleasures of the jolly green woods, he had led them away, except for poor Muley. Muley must have resisted. Perhaps he was the opposition speaker, and got the knife for his brave stand.

The camp was a frightful wreck. Not only were the dogs gone, but everything had been messed up. Every package that could be slashed open with teeth was spilled. The very tent cloth was badly ripped and chewed. So were sleeping bags.

I took stock of the extent of the disaster and then listed details of it. Then I turned about and ran as fast as I could back to the place of the moose.

I found that Massey and Calmont had finished their butchering. Massey sat resting, puffing away at a pipe, while Calmont had his chin propped on his clenched fist, in dark thought. When I told them what I had discovered, Calmont cursed loudly.

"The whole thing is a bust!" he shouted. "I'm sick of it."

"Go home, then," said Massey, after taking a few more puffs on his pipe. "For my part, I'm going to stay here until I get him or until he dies!"

Chapter Twenty-eight
More of Alec's Work

Most men, when they talk about doing or dying, are bluffing, of course. Well, Massey was not. There was no bluff in his whole system. He was simply steel, inside and out.

He had had a number of checks in this business. He had lost the best dog team that I ever saw in the Northland. He had spent a vast amount of invaluable time. He had risked his life over and over again. But now he was settled to the work. Partly, I suppose, the very opposition of hard luck served to make him all the more determined to push through the business. Partly it must have been that he loved Alec the Great in a way that we could not quite understand.

I wondered what Calmont would do, and expected to see him trudge back across country to his shack and resume mining operations. But that was not Calmont's kind. He could stick to disagreeable or hopeless work as long as the next one; and besides, I think he was biding his time and licking his lips for the moment when the dog might be taken by some lucky trick, and the long-postponed fight could take place.

At any rate, though he made no declaration of policy, he stayed on. The first thing we did was to build ourselves a fairly comfortable shelter with the sewed-up remnants of the tent and a lot of logs which we felled in a choice bit of woods. In the clearing that we made before the shack, we put up a meat platform, which was so high that not even a lynx or a fisher could jump to the edge of it. On this we stacked up the frozen moose meat, which made prime eating, I can tell you.

My special job was the light but mean one of stopping the chinks and holes among the log walls of our house with moss, and I was at work for days, doing my clumsy caulking. However, we got the place in fairly good shape, and prepared for a long stay.

Even Massey seemed to have no good plans. When Calmont asked him, he simply replied: "I'm trusting to luck and patience, and that's all. Goodness knows how to go about this. Starvation is the only rope I know of that may be long enough to catch Alec!"

This needed explaining, but Massey pointed out, with a good deal of sense, that wolves and dogs will nearly always establish a regular beat through the woods or over the hills and stick to the particular field which they have outlined. Probably in hard times the range extended a good deal, but it is nearly always run inside of quite distinct limits.

Well, these were hard times for the wolves. We ourselves found little game, but enough to keep our larder well stocked, chiefly because Massey marched for many hours and many miles every day, studying the range of Alec's band, and also shooting everything that he could find. Everything, he said, that he added to our cache on the meat platform was a possibility removed from the teeth and the starved stomachs of Alec and his forces. In fact, he hoped that by sharpening Alec's hunger, he could eventually draw him close to the shack. As a last resort, he was willing to try traps to catch him, at the risk of taking him with a broken leg. But he wanted to wait until the last moment before he did this.

The position we had selected was, according to Massey's explorations, about the center of the wolf range, and, therefore, we were in fairly close striking distance of all their operations.

In the meantime, poor Alec, by his Napoleonic stroke of running off his old companions, the dog team of Massey, had simply loaded himself down with doubled responsibilities. There were now twelve hungry mouths following him and, though we constantly heard the voices of the pack on the blood trail, we guessed that they got little for their trouble, and I've no doubt that rabbits and such lean fare made up most of their meals, such as they were.

Several times we saw them in the distance, and in the glasses of Massey they began to look very tucked-up and gaunted. If there was anything to be hoped for from a partnership with starvation, it looked as though we had it working already.

In the meantime, we sat back at ease and ate our moose meat and simply guarded against wolverines, those expert thieves being the only robbers we had to fear in that part of the woods. The attitude of Massey and Calmont toward one another had not altered. They were simply coldly polite and reserved; and each had an icy look of hatred with which he contemplated the other in unobserved moments. However, I was willing to stack my money on Alec's remaining a free dog. And so long as he ran at large, I saw no chance of the battle taking place. Instinctively, silently, I was praying all day and every day that the fight would not become a fact.

For the more I knew of this pair, the more closely they seemed matched. Massey had the speed of hand, the dauntless spirit, the high courage, and the coldly settled heart of a fighting man. But Calmont balanced these qualities with his enormous strength and a certain brutal savagery which was liable to show him a way to win simply because it would never have occurred to a fair mind like Massey's.

If they fought, I was reasonably sure that Calmont would bring it about that the battle should be hand to hand, and there all his natural advantages of weight and superior height would be sure to tell. That nightmare of expectancy never left me for a moment, night or day.

We had been out there in the woods for about two weeks, eating well and keeping ourselves snug by burning a vast quantity of fuel; and then Alec the Great struck a counter blow, most unexpectedly.

One night I was wakened from sound sleep by muffled noises from the front of the house, though there was enough of a wind whistling to cover any ordinary disturbance. Whatever made those noises, it was not the wind, so I got up and went to the door. This I pushed open and looked onto one of the queerest pictures that any man ever can have seen.

Up there on top of our meat platform was the fine white figure of Alec the Great, and he was dragging great chunks of meat to the edge of the platform and letting them fall into the throats of his followers. This was almost literally true, for the instant that a bit of meat fell, it seemed to be devoured before it had a chance to touch the ground.

It was not so amazing that he had got to the top of the platform. Calmont carelessly had left the ladder standing against it the evening before, forgetful of Alec's ability to climb such things. What startled me was that he should be pulling that meat off the platform and letting it fall to his mates. I dare say that any other animal would have filled his own belly and disregarded its companions. At least, not many outside of the mothers of litters would have had the wit or the impulse to give away fine provisions.

Well, there was Alec up there doing the very thing I have described. It took my breath so that I stared for a moment, incapable of movement. Then I slipped back to Massey and shook him by the shoulder. He waked with a start and grabbed me so hard that he almost broke me in two.

"It's only Joe," I told him. "Alec's outside with his gang. Up on the meat platform. Maybe you can do something about. . . ."

He was at the door before I had finished saying this. On the way, he caught down from the wall a leather rope which he had been making during the past few days, and using as a lariat in practice. And if he could get there close enough to the platform, I was reasonably sure that he would be able to pop the rope onto Alec, and then perhaps have that white treasure for good!

Calmont was up now. The three of us looked out on the destruction of our provisions with no care about them, but only the hope that we could evolve out of this loss a way of recapturing the great dog.

Massey decided that he would go out through the back wall, and that is what he did, pulling up some of the flooring boughs which we used to keep us off the frozen ground, and then burrowing out through the drifted snow beyond.

The other pair of us, still waiting breathlessly inside the doorway, presently made out Massey's stalking through the gloom of the woods at the side of the meat cache.

It looked to me like the end of the chase, and perhaps it might have been, except for a strange thing.

Alec was still pulling the supplies to the edge and letting them topple to the ground, and the rest of the pack were gathered below, snarling softly, now and then, but enjoying that rain of food with burning eyes. One, however, had withdrawn with a prize to the edge of the shrubbery, and this one now started up with a loud, frightened yell.

Once more I could have sworn that it was the old female of whom I've spoken before.

She had spotted Massey in spite of his Indian-like care. And, at that alarm, that wolf-dog pack hit the grit for the shadows as fast as they could scamper.

Alexander the Great, however, delayed a fraction of a second. He picked up a chunk of frozen meat, jumped into the snow with it, and ran after the rest of his boys, carrying his lunch basket with him.

That was an exhibition of good, cool nerve. It was like seeing a man come out of a burning building reading a newspaper on the way, and stopping on the front porch to admire a headline.

Calmont laughed aloud, and I could not help grinning, but poor Massey came in with a desperate face. He actually sat by the fire with his head in his hands, after this, and he said to me that the job was hopeless. They never would capture Alec.

I dared not say that I hoped they wouldn't!

This adventure made me feel that he would have to resort to traps, after all. We had some along with us, carted in from Calmont's shack, and these we oiled up and Calmont himself set them, because he knew the ways of wild animals very well, and had done a good deal of trapping here and there in his day.

Several days after the affair of the meat platform, when we judged that the pack would have empty bellies and eager teeth once more, the traps were placed in well-selected spots, and baited.

The next morning we followed along from trap to trap and found that every one of them had been exposed by scratching in the snow around them.

After this, the wolves had apparently gone on, leaving the traps exposed to ridicule and the open light of the day. Calmont scratched his head and swore that he would try again, and again and again we made the experiment. But it was nearly always with the same result.

Then we saw that the footprints around the traps were always the well-known sign of Alec. The scoundrel was doing all of this detective work which made us feel so helpless and foolish! Presently we began to feel as though Alec were quietly laughing at us, and heartily scorning our foolish efforts to capture him in his own domain. For my part, I had given up the idea entirely.

Then came the great blizzard.

For ten days the wind hardly stopped blowing for a moment. At times, we had a sixty mile wind, and zero weather, which is the coldest thing in the world, so far as I know. There was a great deal of snow that fell during this storm, and at the end of the time, when the gale stopped, we went out into a white world in which Alec was to write a new chapter.

Chapter Twenty-nine
With Teeth Bared

We were a little low in wood for burning, and I went out that morning to get a bit of exercise and also chop down some trees and work them into the right lengths. I picked out some of about the suitable diameter, and soon the axe strokes were going home, while the air filled with the white smoke of the dislodged snow that puffed up from the branches. There was enough wind, now and then, to pick up light whirls of the snow from the ground also, or from the tips of branches, and the air was constantly filled with a dazzling, bright mist. Such an atmospheric condition often brings on snow blindness, I believe. And after working for a time, I was fairly dizzy with the shifting lights and with the surge of blood into my head from the swinging of the axe.

I stepped back, finally, when I had got together a good pile of fuel; and it was then that I saw the rabbit which was eventually to lead on to that adventure.

It looked like a mere puff of snow at first. Then I saw

the dull gleam of its eyes and threw the axe at it.

It hopped a few short bounds away and crouched again. It acted as though it were altogether too weak to move very far.

So I ran suddenly after it, picking up the axe, and the rabbit bobbed up and down, keeping just a little ahead of me, and going with a stagger. It was certainly either sick or exhausted from hunger. Hunger I guessed, because one of the prolonged arctic storms is apt to starve even rabbits.

I went over the top of the next hill and down into the hollow, when, out of the whirling snow mist, leaped a white fox and caught up that rabbit at my very feet.

He carried it off to a very short distance and there actually stopped and began to eat, in full view of me. This amazed me more than ever. They say that animals can tell, sometimes, when men have guns with them and when their hands are empty. I had the light axe, but the fox seemed to know perfectly well that it was a rather silly weapon for distance work.

He went on eating, while I walked slowly toward him.

Two or three times he retreated with the remains of his dinner. But he was reluctant, and he gave me a snaky look and a couple of silent snarls when I walked up on him.

He was about gone with exhaustion and hunger, I could guess. His belly cleaved to his backbone. He was bent like a bow with emptiness and with cold and looked brittle and stiff.

The way he put himself outside that rabbit was worth seeing and, when he had finished it, he did not skulk off, but licked his red chops and began to eye me!

I tried to laugh at the impudence of him, but I found that I was getting the creeps. A fox is not a very big creature and, minus its beautiful coat, it is usually a poor little starveling. But that fox seemed to grow bigger and bigger.

Finally, I again threw my axe at it.

The beast let the axe fly over its head without so much as budging and, staring at me, it licked its red lips again. I was to it what a moose would be to a man—a mountain of meat, and somehow I knew that that beast was coveting the lord of creation as represented by me.

I stepped back. I turned on it. The little brute snarled at me with the utmost hate, and would not budge.

This angered me so much that I shouted, and ran forward, after which my fox shrank a little to the side, and remained there, snarling, its snaky bright eyes on my throat. I was almost afraid to pick up my axe, for fear I would be rushed as I bent forward; but when I had the axe in my hand, I decided that I would waste no more time out here getting myself frozen, and instead go back toward the house, in the hope of luring this vengeful fox after me.

But the matter of the fox was taken off my hands exactly as the matter of the rabbit had been. Out of the snow mist, shining and thick, a stream of gaunt, gray forms came streaking, with a shining white body in the forefront. The fox whirled about and started to scamper, but he had waited too long in his interest in me.

Before he could get into his running stride, Alec the Great struck him down before my eyes, and the poor fox screamed for one half second as the gray flood closed over him.

I dare say that between the time the meat was stolen from the platform and the time this fox was pulled down that pack had not touched food of any kind. At least, they looked it, with their hollowed stomachs and arched backs, and their eyes were stains of red, glaring frightfully.

"Alec!" I loudly shouted. "Alec, Alec!"

At my voice, that wave of gray parted from above the bones of the fox and then closed together once more over it. They, also, seemed to know pretty well that even if I were a man, yet I had no gun with me. I whirled the axe and shouted again, without getting any more response than if I had shouted at the arctic trees in their winter silence.

This frightened me suddenly.

There are stories about hungry wolves and overly confident men. You will hear those stories occasionally, in camp, when the beasts are howling far away on a blood trail. They make bad yarns and haunt one at night.

Well, I backed away from that gang and then turned and started for the house. I had barely got started, when I heard a rushing sound behind me, something like that of a gust of wind through trees. I looked back over my shoulder. It was no wind. It was the noise of the loose, dry snow, whipped up by the running legs of thirteen dogs and wolves, for that whole pack was coming for me, and Alec the Great was in the lead, with the ugly wolf bitch at his side.

Fear did not numb me, luckily. There was a patch of trees standing in a huddle to one side of me, and I got to those trees as fast as a greyhound could have jumped the distance. They would guard my back, if only I could fight off the enemy from the front! I shouted with all my might, but—perhaps it was the sight of the snow fog in the air—I was sure that my voice would never reach to the ears of my friends in the house. If only the wolves would howl.

But they did not. They sat down in a semicircle before me, while Alec the Great, according to his usual tactics, marched up and down the line, marshaling his forces, planning his wicked devices.

I say wolves, though most of them were merely huskies, but they looked all wolf, now, and they certainly acted all wolf, as well. Their red eyes had evil in them, and there was more evil in Alec, our former pet, than in any of the rest of the lot.

Suddenly I said: "Alec, old boy, you ought to remember me. Yonder in Nome I got you out of as bad a mess as this, when the dog team was about to mob you!"

Now, when I said this, I give you my word that that beautiful white brute stopped in his slinking walk and turned his head toward me, with ears so pricked and with eyes so bright that I could have sworn that he understood every syllable that I was speaking.

He waited there, with a forepaw raised, and smiling a red, wolfish smile. I was understood by him, he seemed to be saying; but he was not at all convinced that he intended to return good for good.

While I was talking to Alec, the real mischief started. The old bitch had worked herself close to me through the snow, wriggling like a seal and unnoticed by me until she rose from the ground at my very feet and tried for my throat. She would have got it, too, except that I jerked down on the axe from my shoulder with an instinctive, not an aimed, blow that went straight home between her eyes. It split her skull. She struck me heavily on the chest, knocking me back against the trees, and then fell dead at my feet, while I, gasping, and shouting louder than ever for help, swung the axe again and prepared to meet the rush.

It came.

One of the wolves, a big, strong male, rushed in on me, as though trying to take advantage of any confusion I might be in after repulsing the attack of the bitch. I made a half turn and gave it to him alongside the head.

It did not kill him. It merely slashed him badly, and made him spring for my throat.

Then they settled down in their semicircle again, and once more they waited.

Alec set the example of patience by lying prone on his belly in the snow and commencing to bite out the ice from between his toes. Only the wolf which had been wounded stood stiffly in place, his eyes red and green by turns, like lights on a railroad, except that green was the danger signal, here.

All that scene is burned into my mind, though I thought at the time that I would never remember anything except the wolfish eyes. Fear and horror came over me in waves. Sometimes I thought that I might faint. The dread of this kept me strung taut. And I remember how a puff of wind opened the snow mist before me and gave me a sight of the whole hollow, and the dark forest beyond, while a hope leaped up for an instant in my breast, and was gone again as the mist closed in once more.

I saved up my voice, as it were, and shouted from time to time, pitching the notes very high, and then lower, wondering if any sound might come to the cabin where two strong men and rifles were ready to scatter ten times as many wolves as these like nothing at all.

As I shouted, I remembered that the wolves and dogs would cant their heads a little and listen like connoisseurs of music. If it came to making a noise, I was an amateur compared to these musicians of the wilderness. This comparison struck me at the time and almost made me smile, which shows how oddly we can detach ourselves from ourselves.

Well, Alec was the one who brought me down.

The treacherous dog must have been planning it carefully in his almost human brain. He was lying there licking his forelegs one instant and the next moment he was in at me like a flash. I suppose he had gathered his hind legs carefully beneath him for the spring, while he maintained that sham in front to deceive me. And deceive me he did, and most perfectly.

The first thing I knew that white slash was on me.

He did not go for the throat. Instead, he used the trick that Massey had taught him with such care in the days of his puppyhood. He simply gave me his shoulder at the knees, and the force of that blow laid me flat with a jolt that almost winded me.

I jerked my arms across my face and throat, instead of striking out. I heard a deep, moaning growl which I supposed was the joy note from those hungry vandals.

Well, it makes me blush to relate that I closed my eyes and simply waited that frightful split second for my murder to commence, knowing that something was standing over me, snarling frightfully. Teeth clashed. Something tugged at my clothes.

And then I opened my cowardly eyes and saw that Alec the Great was standing over me, not trying for my throat, but keeping back the wolf pack with his bared teeth!

Chapter Thirty
For Life and Death

People have tried to explain all this to me. They have said that, of course, scent is the keenest sense in a dog or a wolf, and that it was not until he was close on me, this cold, blowing day, that Alec the Great was able to note my scent and record me in his memory as an old friend. Some people have even said that it was all a game on his part. But then, they were not there to see the look in his eyes before he jumped in at me. However, I never have been convinced by any of these attempted explanations. They may all be correct, but I suppose I prefer to keep the thing a miracle.

When I looked up and saw how the battle was going, you can imagine that I got to my feet in double-quick time. I scooped up the axe which had fallen from my hand into the deep snow, only the end of the haft sticking out above the surface.

My troubles were not over. The pack had yielded ground for a moment at the strange spectacle of its leader going over to the enemy, but hunger was more eloquent than their respect for the teeth of Alec the Great.

They came bundling in toward us in a tumult. And Alec?

Why he fought them off like a master, with my help. I kept my axe swinging as hard and as fast as I could and, as the wolves swerved this way and that from the blade—a tooth which they learned quickly to respect— Alec flashed out at them like a sword from its scabbard, and cutting right and left was back again in the shallow shelter which I made for him.

That dog moved as quickly as a striking snake. Even the real wild wolves were slow compared with him. And this again, of course, was the result of man-training, plus native ability and brains. He seemed to think out things in a human manner. In parrying those attacks, for instance, he gave almost all of his attention to the big gray wolf which already had been slashed by the axe blade. That fellow was the champion of the old brigade, one might say, and he led the way for the rest, feinting in very cleverly, and always trying to get to me, as though he understood perfectly well that what made the strength of Alec and me was our partnership, and that I was the weaker of the two. Half a dozen times his long fangs were not an inch from my face, for he was always trying for my throat.

And Alec, making this his chief enemy, finally found a chance to rip that timber wolf right across the belly as he was jumping up and in.

The wounded beast hit the ground and went off to a little distance before it lay down on the snow.

Then it got up, leaving a pool of red where it had lain, and went off with small, slow steps. I guessed that it was bleeding to death rapidly and wanted to get into the dark of the forest before its fellows found out its bad condition.

Well, it had no luck. It was leaving a broad trail behind it, and famine and the bad luck they were having with Alec and me made the rest of the pack swerve away from us and head after their wounded companion.

When he saw them coming, he quickened his pace into a wretched, short-striding gallop. He got to the shadow of the woods a bit before the others, but I knew that they must have been on him in a swarming crowd, a moment later. Yet there was no sound to tell of it. Hunger shut their throats. Just as they had swarmed silently around me, so they must have swarmed silently around that wounded comrade, tearing him to bits.

For my part, I cared not a whit what became of them and all the rest of the wolves and huskies in the world, for I was down on my knees in the snow with my arms around Alec the Great hugging him against my breast like a long-lost brother.

His reaction to this was very odd.

First, he shuddered and snarled, and I could feel and see his hair bristling along his back. But, after a moment, Alec became a different creature.

He had had a long contact with the wilderness, of course, and I suppose his long association with Calmont had given humanity a black eye with him for the time being. But as I talked to Alec and caressed him, finally his tail began to wag. He kissed my face and, sitting down in the snow before me, he laughed in my face, with his wise head canted a little to one side, exactly as he used to carry it in the old days, when he was asking what he should do next.

This delighted me wonderfully, and I began to laugh until the tears stung my face.

However, I had to get home quickly.

Half a dozen times, the cutting fangs of those desperadoes had touched my clothes, and with the next grip huge rents and tears appeared. These let in the cold on me, like water through a sieve, and I was shuddering from head to foot.

So I headed up the hill, my heart very high, you may be sure, and my head turned to watch Alec.

Well, he came right up after me until we reached the ridge of the hill, with the cabin in full view on its side. There Alec the Great sat down and would not budge for a long moment.

He stared at the house, then he turned his head and looked toward the woods and, if ever a strong brain turned two ideas back and forth visibly, it was Alec there on the hill, looking down, as I felt, at all humanity, all civilization, and calmly asking himself if the penalties were worth the pleasures compared with the wild, free life of a king of the woods.

I called him. I coaxed him.

Finally, he jumped up as though he had known what to do all the time, but had merely been resting. And with Alec at my heels, I went on to the cabin and thrust open the clumsy door which we had made to seal the entrance.

It seemed dim inside, and the air was rank with great swirls of pipe smoke, and the reeking fumes of frying bacon. It was very close, and the air was bad, but it was warm. However, no conqueror ever walked into a castle in a conquered city with a greater feeling of pride than I had as I stalked in with Alec at my heels.

Calmont saw us first, and groaned out an oath which held all his amazement in it. He stood back against the wall, still gasping and muttering, while Alec crouched on the threshold and snarled in reply. Those green eyes of his plainly told what he thought of Calmont and all of Calmont's kind!

Massey, when he saw what I had with me, made no remark at all. But he looked at me like a fellow seeing a ghost. It was a moment before Alec spotted him, and then he crawled across the floor, dragging himself almost on his belly, until he was close. Once in range, he fairly leaped at Massey, and in another moment they were wrestling all over the floor of that cabin, and threatening to wreck the place.

It was just one of their little games but, since they last played it together, Alec had almost doubled his strength. He was a handful, I can tell you!

At this game I looked on with a wide grin, but Calmont saw nothing jolly about it at all. It meant that the dog was back, and that he was still as much of an outcast as ever. It was again Calmont against the world of Massey, Alec the Great, and me.

Poor Calmont! Looking back at him as he was then, I can look a little deeper into his nature than I thought I could at that time. That reunion of Massey with the dog was a grand thing to watch, I thought, and I laughed rather drunkenly—with a mug of coffee steaming in one hand, and a chunk of meat in the other—while Calmont turned his back on the dog and the man and paid his attention to me.

He found some cuts and tied them for me. I wished, then, that there had been twice as many cuts, for Calmont put his great hand on my shoulder and said: "Kid, you're a good game one! A right good game one!"

It was the very first kind word that he had ever spoken to me. It was almost the first time that he had so much as taken notice of my existence, and I was puffed up so big that I would have floated at a touch.

I felt that I was a man, now, and a mighty important man, too, having done myself what the pair of them had been unable to accomplish. It didn't occur to me that the whole affair had been accident. Boys never think out the discreditable and chance parts of an adventure. In a way I think that the young are apt to live on the impressions which they give older people. I had made a great impression this day, and it brimmed my cup with happiness.

When things settled down, Massey, sitting on the floor with big Alec laughing silently beside him, asked me for the whole story. I pretended to be reluctant to speak, but I let them drag the yarn out of me, speaking short and carelessly, but all the while almost bursting with my pride; and so I went from the rabbit to the fox, and from the fox to the wolves. And Massey listened and nodded with shining eyes.

He did not commend me openly. But then he was not the man to do that before a comparative stranger like Calmont. Whatever I did that was worth doing, I knew that Massey took as much joy in it as I did myself. He was that kind of a man, but he spoke his praise in one or two short words, quietly, when I was alone with him. It was one of the qualities that made me love him.

When I got on to the end of the story, and how Alec had hesitated on the top of the hill, Massey simply said: "Well, he'll never hesitate again." Afterward he added: "I make out that you left one wolf dead there on the snow, old son?"

Yes, I said that the bitch had been stretched dead there.

"But lad," said Massey, "that means that you just walked off and left a perfectly good wolf skin behind you?"

I said that was it. I was not interested in skinning wolves, just then.

"Trot off there and get it, then," said Massey. "You'll want to keep that skin, with the slit in the skull, and all. It'll give a point to the telling of this story, one day, for your friends and your children, and all such. Trot off and get that, and start in hoping right now that the pack hasn't returned to dine off that dead body!''

The idea seemed perfectly clear to me. I jumped up without a word, and without another thought, and tore out of that shack like mad, to get to the place before the wolves came back.

I got across the hill, and breathed more easily when I saw the body stretched there, dark against the snow, and the wind riffling in the long fur.

I had my knife out as I got up to the body, but when I turned the wolf on her back and was about to make the first cut I remembered, suddenly, the other half of what was to come.

Calmont and Massey, and the agreement they had made!

Then I saw, with blinding clearness that it was simply a trick of that clever Massey to get me out of the way. I was to be shunted to one side and, while I collected my foolish wolf skin, they were back there fighting for life and death—and the ownership of Alec.

Chapter Thirty-one
Onward, and Fast!

As fast as I could leg it, I hurried back toward the cabin. The wind had dropped to nothing, but the snow was falling very fast, filling the air with a white, thick dust. There was one comfort—that I heard not a sound from the direction of the cabin, and this I took to be a great and sure sign, because when two such giants met, I could not help feeling that there would be an uproar which could be heard for tens of miles away.

Quite winded, I reached the upper rim of the hill and saw the dull outlines of the cabin looming before me through the shimmer of the mist of snowfall. All seemed peaceful to me, and I stopped for an instant to draw breath; and all at once I wished that I had not left the wolf, but that I had done my work before I came back to the cabin, carrying the wolf skin for which I had been sent.

I was embarrassed, ill at ease, and shifting from one foot to the other. As people do in such a state of mind,

I shifted my glance to the side, and there I saw in the bottom of the hollow what looked to me like two giants breathing and tossing about a white vapor.

I looked again, and then all the dream-like quality of this scene vanished, for I knew that it was Calmont and Massey fighting for their lives—and Alec!

Where was Alexander the Great?

I saw him then, on a short chain fastened outside the cabin, and at the same time I heard him bark twice or thrice in a mournful, inquiring tone. As if he asked what those two men were doing at the lower end of the hollow.

It struck me at the time as rather a ghastly thing that the two of them should have decided to fight it out with the dog there to look on. But while I thought of this, I began to run toward the pair of them, not really hoping that I could stop their battle, but because I could not remain at a distance. For it suddenly came home to me that though I loved Massey, I could not look on the death of Calmont with equanimity. I remembered, then, and never was to forget, how he had put his heavy hand on my shoulder and said: "You're game!"

Other men in my life have occasionally said pleasant things to me, but not even from Massey did I ever receive such an accolade.

So I lunged down the hollow with my heart in my mouth.

I could distinguish them at once, partly by the superior size of Calmont and partly by the superior speed of Massey. He was like a cat on his feet, and even the thickness of the snow could not altogether mask his celerity. The snow, too, was kicked up in light, fluffy clouds around the site of the struggle, and yet through this glimmering, white mist I followed every act of the two battlers.

I saw Calmont run in, like a bull, head down, terrible

in his force and weight; and I saw Massey leap aside like a light-footed wolf. Oh, that gave me hope for Massey! Like a wolf in speed, like a wolf in action, and like a wolf, also, in the ability to hurt terribly when the opportunity came.

It came at that very moment.

I could not see the strokes that he delivered, but distinctly through the mist I saw Calmont turn and strive to come in again, and saw him checked and wavering before what he met.

Of course, his plan was clear. He was a great wrestler, equipped for the game by his gigantic muscles, and what he wanted was to close with his old bunkie and, gripping him close, get a strangle hold.

It seemed to me that I could tell the whole argument— how Massey had held out for knife or gun, and how Calmont had insisted grimly that it should be hand to hand, where his weight and superior strength would tell.

Well, I knew the fiery disposition of Massey too well to doubt what the outcome of such an argument would be even before I saw the actual result of it. He could not decline a dare. He had to fight, if a fight were offered, no matter what the odds.

So there they were, meeting each other according to Calmont's desire. Yet it was not going, apparently, as Calmont would have wished. He was baffled before those educated fists of Massey.

I saw him rush again, and again I saw him go back from Massey, and knew that blows were propelling him.

At this I tried to cry out, and either my excitement or my breathlessness stopped my voice before it could issue from my lips.

Running down at full speed, I was much closer when I saw Massey, in turn, take the aggressive.

It was a beautiful thing to see him dart in, wavering

like a wind-blown leaf, but hitting, I have no doubt, like
the stroke of sledgehammers, for that monstrous Calmont reeled before him again, and suddenly there was
no Calmont any longer!

He was down, I saw next. He was more than half-
buried in the loose snow which they had kicked up into
a dense cloud about them.

And now would Massey leap in to take advantage of
a fallen enemy?

No, there was something knightly about Massey. Such
a thing was simply out of his mind, and he kept his
distance while Calmont struggled clumsily to his feet.

I should say that he was not actually on his feet, but
only on his knees as I came hurtling down the hill toward them. I ran right straight between them and, as I
did so, I saw that Calmont had pulled out from beneath
his clothes that revolver whose possession he had denied. He pulled it out, and through the snow mist I saw
him leveling it at Massey, and I saw the red-stained face
of Calmont there behind the gun.

I shouted at him: "Calmont! Calmont! Fight fair!"

I shouted at him, I say, just as I came between him
and his enemy, and made it so that at that moment he
pulled the trigger.

At this time I don't remember hearing the gun at all.
I only saw the flash of the powder and a heavy impact
struck me in the body.

That I remember, and with sickening distinctness the
knowledge that I had been shot. The force of the blow
whirled me half around. I staggered and was about to
fall when I saw Calmont, through a haze of terror and
of snow mist, leap upward from the ground and throw
the revolver he had used far away, and come rushing in
to me with his arms thrown out.

He caught me up. It was like being seized in the noose

of steel cables. That man was a gorilla and did not know his strength compared with the frailty of ordinary human flesh and bone.

He caught me up, and I looked to his face and saw it through the swirling darkness that comes at fainting.

When I next saw with any distinctness, there was a frightful, burning pain in my side, and I remember that my throat was hard and aching, as if I had been screaming. And I suppose that was exactly what I was doing.

I looked up and saw Calmont's face above me, contorted like a fiend's. I thought, in my agony, that Calmont was a demon, appointed by Fate to torment me.

At that moment, I heard him cry out: "I'll hold him, Hugh, and you do the thing. I can't bear it!"

Then I saw that Hugh Massey was holding me, and that he was transferring me to Calmont's arms.

I remember feeling that everything would have to turn out all right, in spite of pain and torment, so long as Massey was there. He was not the sort to deny an old friend and companion. He would rather die than do such a thing, but there was a profound wonder that the pair of them could have been working over one cause, and that cause myself!

This blackness into which I had dropped thinned again, later on, and I found myself looking up toward the ceiling of the room of the cabin. There was a vast weakness which, like a tangible thing, was floating back and forth inside me.

And then I heard the voice of Calmont, low, and hard, and strained, as he said: "Massey, I want you to hear something."

To this Massey said: "I've heard enough from you. I most certainly wish that I could even forget the thought of you!"

"Aye," said Calmont, "and so do I. I wish that I

could forget, but I can't. I've been a mean one and a low one. I was being fair-licked, today, and I took an underhand way of pulling myself even with you. You've been licking me twice, Massey, when I've tried an extra trick, outside of the game. And if we fought again, I couldn't promise that I'd still be fair. But I want to say this to you. . . ."

"I've heard enough of your sayings," said Hugh Massey.

"You've heard enough, and I'm tired of my own voice," said Calmont, "but what I want to say is this: Everything is yours. You've beaten me in everything, I dunno how. But it's because you're the better man, I reckon. Strong hands is one thing but goodness is another, too.

"I've missed that out of my figgering!" said Calmont, continuing. "I've figgered that I could take as much as I could grab . . . and carry. But I've been wrong. You're a smaller man, but you've got Marjorie, and you have got Alec, and the kid there loves you like a brother. A good, game kid," said Calmont.

I half closed my eyes, for it was a sweet thing to hear. I hardly cared whether I lived or died. I was too sick to care, much. And that is the consolation of sickness, to be sure! The fellow who is about to die is generally more than half numb and he does not suffer as much as he seems to.

"Shut up," said Massey. "You'll be waking the kid."

"Aye," said Calmont softly, "I'll shut up. Only . . . I wanted to say something. . . ."

"I'm not interested in your sayings," said Massey.

A little strength came back to me at this. I managed to call out: "Hugh!"

There was simply a swish of wind, he came so fast.

He stood above me and looked down at me with the sort of a smile that a man generally is ashamed to show a man. He keeps it for children and women.

"Aye, partner," says he.

I closed my eyes and let the echo of that go kindly through me. "Partner" he had called me, and no other man in the world, I knew, ever had been called that by Massey, except Arnie Calmont himself, in the old days. Old days that never would come again.

"Hugh," I said, "will you give me your hand?"

He grabbed my hand. His grip was terrible to feel.

"Are you feeling bad?" he says to me. "Oh, Calmont, you'll pay for this!"

Suddenly there was the terrible wolfish face of Calmont on the other side of me, leaning above. Except that he didn't look wolfish then, only mightily strained and sick.

"I'll pay on earth and hereafter!" said Calmont.

I stared up at them. I felt that I was dying, but I wanted only the strength to say to them what was in my mind.

They both leaned close. Massey suddenly slumped to his knees, with a loud bang, and gently slid an arm under my head.

"Hold hard, old boy," he said to me.

"I'm holding . . . hard," I said. "Will you listen?"

"Aye," he said, "I'll listen."

"Yes," said Calmont, "and more than that!"

Calmont had hold of one of my hands. Hugh had hold of the other. I pulled my two hands together. For I saw, then, that nothing in the world could stop them from killing one another. Most of the bitterness had been on Calmont's part, before this. But afterward, it would be Massey who would never rest until he had squared accounts.

Alec, who always knew when something important was being said, came and laid his head on my shoulder in a strange way.

"Calmont . . . Massey," I panted. "Don't let me go black again before I've told you. . . ."

"Don't tell us anything," said Calmont. "Close your eyes. Rest up. You're going to be fine. You hear me? You're right as can be, kid!"

I closed my eyes, as he said, because it seemed to rest me and to save my strength.

"Partners," I said, "it looks to me as though you two would have to team together. You started together. You stayed fast together, till Alec budged you apart. Together, you could beat a hundred, but apart you'll only serve to kill each other. I'm sort of fading out. But before I finish, I'd like to see you shake hands and see that you're friends again."

"I'll see him hanged," said Massey in a terrible voice. "I'll see him hanged before I'll take his hand. I'll sooner take his throat!"

Well, he meant it. He was that kind of man.

I looked up at them, but I was dumb, and black was floating and then whirling before my eyes.

Calmont held out his hand.

"Aye, Hugh," he said, "whatever you please, afterward. But this is for the kid."

At that, I saw Massey grip the hand of Calmont in both of his. They stared at each other. Never were there two such men in the world as that pair who stood over me there in the cabin, with Alec whining pitifully at my ear.

"Maybe the kid's right, and we've both been wrong," said Massey suddenly. "Maybe we've always needed each other! Here's my hand for good and all, Arnie, and hang me if I ever go back on my word!"

"Your word," said Calmont, "is a pile better than gold, to me. And this is the best minute I've ever seen. Mind the kid . . . mind. . . ."

The last of this, however, came dimly to me. I felt a vast happiness coming over me, but the darkness increased, and a sudden pain in the side stabbed inward until it reached my heart, and then the rest of the world was completely lost.

But I think that if I had died then I would have died happily, so far as happy deaths are possible, with a feeling that I had managed a great thing before the end of me.

At any rate, the world vanished from before my senses, and did not come back to me until I saw, over my head, the cold, bright faces of the stars, and heard Hugh Massey giving brief, low-voiced orders to dogs.

"How is he?" asked Massey from a distance.

"His heart is going still . . . but dead slow," said the voice of Calmont just above me. "Go on, and go fast, and Heaven help us!"

Chapter Thirty-two
King of the Road

Sometimes I think when I remember that ride through the winter cold and through the ice of the wind, that it could not be, and that no man—or boy—could have lived through what flowed through me, at that time; but the facts are there for men to know, in spite of the way the doctor cursed and opened his eyes when he looked at me in Dawson.

What had happened, I learned afterward from Massey, was that Alec, being left free to run as he would while Calmont and Hugh struggled to keep a spark of life in me during those first days, had gradually hunted through the woods until he called back to him with his hunting song the lost members of the team of Calmont, and the fragments of Massey's own string. They came back, and they settled in around the house as if they had never been away. That was the influence of Alec, who had driven them wild and who was able, in this manner, to tame them again.

I never could say whether he was more man than dog, or more dog than man, or more wizard than either.

At any rate, the time came when Calmont and Massey decided that they could not keep the failing life in me with their meager resources, and so they took the great chance, and the only chance, of taking me off to Dawson.

I wish that I had had consciousness enough to have seen and appreciated that ride down to Dawson. It passed to me like a frightfully bad dream, for I was tormented with pain, and I know that I must have cried out in delirium many a time, and wakened, setting my teeth over another yell.

But how much I should have liked to see Calmont herding that team forward, and Massey breaking the trail, or Calmont driving, and Massey beside me.

They were men. They were hard men. They were the very hardest men that I ever saw in all that cold, hard country. But they treated me as if each of them were my blood brother.

When they got me down to Dawson and took me into the doctor's office, I came to for fair, and I wish that I hadn't, for I had to endure the probing of the wound, with both Calmont and Massey looking on.

If they had not been there, I could have yelled my head off, which would have been a relief; but both of them were standing by, and I had to grip my jaws hard together and endure the misery, and a mighty sick business that was.

I remember that Calmont assured the doctor that, if I died, there would be one doctor fewer in Dawson; and I remember that Massey told him that if I got well there would be a certain number of pounds of gold. . . .

But the doctor cursed them both—which is a way that

doctors have, and assured them that he cared not a rap for the pair of them, multiplied by ten.

Well, I was put away in a bed, and gradually life began to come back to me, though the doctor himself assured me that there was not the slightest good reason for me coming back to the land of the living, and that according to all the books I should have died. He even made a chart to show me all the vital parts that the bullet had gone through.

However, here I am to write the end to this story.

I write it, however, not in Alaska's blues and whites, but among Arizona's own twilit purples, with the voice of Marjorie Massey singing in the kitchen, and the voice of Hugh sounding in the corral, where he's breaking a three-year-old, and I can hear the yipping of Alexander the Great.

I get up to look out the window, and see Alec perched on top of the fence, laughing a red laugh at the world, of which he knows that he is the master, the undisputed king of the road, boss of the ranch dogs for fifty miles around, slayer of coyotes, foxes, and even the tall timber wolves. He goes where he pleases. He opens doors to go and come. He thinks nothing of waking the entire household in the middle of the night. He knows that for him there is not in the world a stick, a stone, a whip, or a harsh word.

I think of this as I see the big rascal standing on the fence and then go back to my chair and take from my pocket a yellow paper. It is fraying at the creases as I unfold it and read in a heavy scrawl what Calmont left behind him when he departed one night from among us, after coming all the way from the white North to stand behind Hugh at his wedding as best man:

"God be good to all of you, but you'll be better off without me."

About the Author

Max Brand™ is the best-known pen name of Frederick Faust, creator of Dr. Kildare™, Destry, and many other fictional characters popular with readers and viewers worldwide. Faust wrote for a variety of audiences in many genres. His enormous output, totaling approximately thirty million words or the equivalent of 530 ordinary books, covered nearly every field: crime, fantasy, historical romance, espionage, Westerns, science fiction, adventure, animal stories, love, war, and fashionable society, big business and big medicine. Eighty motion pictures have been based on his work along with many radio and television programs. For good measure he also published four volumes of poetry. Perhaps no other author has reached more people in more different ways.

Born in Seattle in 1892, orphaned early, Faust grew up in the rural San Joaquin Valley of California. At Berkeley he became a student rebel and one-man literary movement, contributing prodigiously to all campus publications. Denied a degree because of unconventional conduct, he embarked on a series of adventures culminating in New York City where, after a period of near starvation, he received simultaneous recognition as a serious poet and successful popular-prose writer. Later, he traveled widely, making his home in New York, then in Florence, and finally in Los Angeles.

Once the United States entered the Second World War, Faust abandoned his lucrative writing career and his work as a screenwriter to serve as a war correspondent with the infantry in Italy, despite his fifty-one years and a bad heart. He was killed during a night attack on a hilltop village held by the German army. New books based on magazine serials or unpublished manuscripts continue to appear. Alive and dead he has averaged a new one every four months for seventy-five years. In the U.S. alone nine publishers issue his work, plus many more in foreign countries. Yet, only recently have the full dimensions of this extraordinarily versatile and prolific writer come to be recognized and his stature as a protean literary figure in the 20th century acknowledged. His popularity continues to grow throughout the world.

RONICKY DOONE'S TREASURE

MAX BRAND

"Brand is a topnotcher!"
—*New York Times*

A horsebreaker, mischief-maker, and adventurer by instinct, Ronicky Doone dares every gunman in the West to outdraw him—and he always wins. But nothing prepares him for the likes of Jack Moon and his wild bunch. Hunting down a fortune in hidden loot, the desperadoes swear to string up or shoot down anyone who stands in their way. When Doone crosses their path, he needs a shootist's skill and a gambler's luck to survive, and if that isn't enough, his only reward will be a pine box.

_3748-3 $3.99 US/$4.99 CAN

Dorchester Publishing Co., Inc.
P.O. Box 6640
Wayne, PA 19087-8640

Please add $1.75 for shipping and handling for the first book and $.50 for each book thereafter. NY, NYC, and PA residents, please add appropriate sales tax. No cash, stamps, or C.O.D.s. All orders shipped within 6 weeks via postal service book rate. Canadian orders require $2.00 extra postage and must be paid in U.S. dollars through a U.S. banking facility.

Name_____

Address_____

City_____ State_____ Zip_____

I have enclosed $_____ in payment for the checked book(s).

Payment <u>must</u> accompany all orders. ☐ Please send a free catalog.

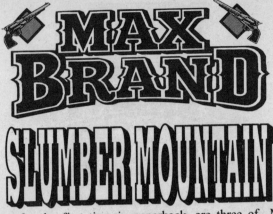

MAX BRAND

SLUMBER MOUNTAIN

Here, for the first time in paperback, are three of Max Brand's best short novels, all restored to their original glory from Brand's own typescripts and presented just as he intended. "Outland Crew" is an exciting tale of gold fever and survival in a frontier mining town. In "The Coward," a man humiliated in a gunfight finds a fiendishly clever way of exacting revenge. And in "Slumber Mountain," Brand presents a harrowing story of man versus the wilderness as a trapper fights for his life against the mighty wolf known as Silver King.

___4442-0 $4.99 US/$5.99 CAN

OUTLAWS
ALL

From Alaska to the Southwest, Max Brand, the master of the Western tale, brings the excitement of the frontier to life like no one else. His characters live, breathe, struggle and triumph in a world so real you can hear the creaking of the saddle leather. Gathered in this collection are three classic short novels by Brand, all filled with the adventure and heroism, the guts and the gunsmoke, that made the West what it was.

___4398-X $4.50 US/$5.50 CAN

Dorchester Publishing Co., Inc.
P.O. Box 6640
Wayne, PA 19087-8640

Please add $1.75 for shipping and handling for the first book and $.50 for each book thereafter. NY, NYC, and PA residents, please add appropriate sales tax. No cash, stamps, or C.O.D.s. All orders shipped within 6 weeks via postal service book rate. Canadian orders require $2.00 extra postage and must be paid in U.S. dollars through a U.S. banking facility.

Name_____
Address_____
City_____State_____Zip_____
I have enclosed $_____ in payment for the checked book(s).
Payment <u>must</u> accompany all orders. ☐ Please send a free catalog.
CHECK OUT OUR WEBSITE! www.dorchesterpub.com

MAX BRAND

THE RETURN OF FREE RANGE LANNING

The people of Martindale have taken Andy Lanning and turned him from a decent young man into a desperate, tough gunman. After shooting a man in a fight he didn't want any part of, Andy had to head for the mountains. He's learned to survive—and now he is headed back home, back to Martindale to claim the woman he loves. But a lot of people in town believe Andy's a killer, and they aren't exactly waiting with open arms. If he plans to stay around, Andy has a lot to prove...both to the town and to himself.

___4294-0 $4.50 US/$5.50 CAN

"Max Brand is a topnotcher!"
—The New York Times

King Charlie. Lord of sagebrush and saddle leather, leader of outlaws and renegades, Charlie rules the wild territory with a fist of iron. But the times are changing, the land is being tamed, and men like Charlie are quickly fading into legend. Before his empire disappears into the sunset, Charlie swears he'll pass his legacy on to only one man: the ornery cuss who can claim it with bullets—or blood.

_4182-0 $4.50 US/$5.50 CAN

Red Devil of the Range. Only two things in this world are worth a damn to young Ever Winton—his Uncle Clay and the mighty Red Pacer, the wildest, most untamable piece of horseflesh in the West. Then in one black hour they are both gone—and Ever knows he has to get them both back. He'll do whatever it takes, even if it costs his life—or somebody else's.

_4122-7 $4.50 US/$5.50 CAN

Dorchester Publishing Co., Inc.
P.O. Box 6640
Wayne, PA 19087-8640

Please add $1.75 for shipping and handling for the first book and $.50 for each book thereafter. NY, NYC, and PA residents, please add appropriate sales tax. No cash, stamps, or C.O.D.s. All orders shipped within 6 weeks via postal service book rate. Canadian orders require $2.00 extra postage and must be paid in U.S. dollars through a U.S. banking facility.

Name_____

Address_____

City_____ State_____ Zip_____

I have enclosed $_____ in payment for the checked book(s).

Payment <u>must</u> accompany all orders. ❏ Please send a free catalog.

THE WHITE WOLF

MAX BRAND

"Brand is a topnotcher!"
—New York Times

Tucker Crosden breeds his dogs to be champions. Yet even by the frontiersman's brutal standards, the bull terrier called White Wolf is special. With teeth bared and hackles raised, White Wolf can brave any challenge the wilderness throws in his path. And Crosden has great plans for the dog until it gives in to the blood-hungry laws of nature. But Crosden never reckons that his prize animal will run at the head of a wolf pack one day—or that a trick of fate will throw them together in a desperate battle to the death.

__3870-6 $4.50 US/$5.50 CAN

MAX BRAND

TROUBLE IN TIMBERLINE

"Brand is a topnotcher!"
—New York Times

Barney Dwyer is too big and too awkward to be much good around a ranch. But foreman Dan Peary has the perfect job for him. It seems Peary's son has joined up with a ruthless gang in the mountain town of Timberline, and Peary wants Barney to bring the no-account back, alive. Before long, Barney finds himself up to his powerful neck in trouble—both from gunslingers who defy the law and tin stars who are sworn to uphold it!

_3848-X $4.50 US/$5.50 CAN

THE BELLS
OF
SAN FILIPO

"Brand is a topnotcher!"   *—New York Times*

Year in and year out, Jim Gore wanders the barren hills of the Southwest, dreaming of mining the mother lode. Yet for all his schemes and hard work, the cunning saddle bum never figures on an earthquake uncovering a huge treasure in silver—and plunging him neck deep in dollars and danger. It seems that Gore isn't the only hombre who has a claim on the loot, and if he ever runs out of bullets, he won't be the only fortune hunter buried in the ghost town called San Filipo.

_3819-6 $3.99 US/$4.99 CAN